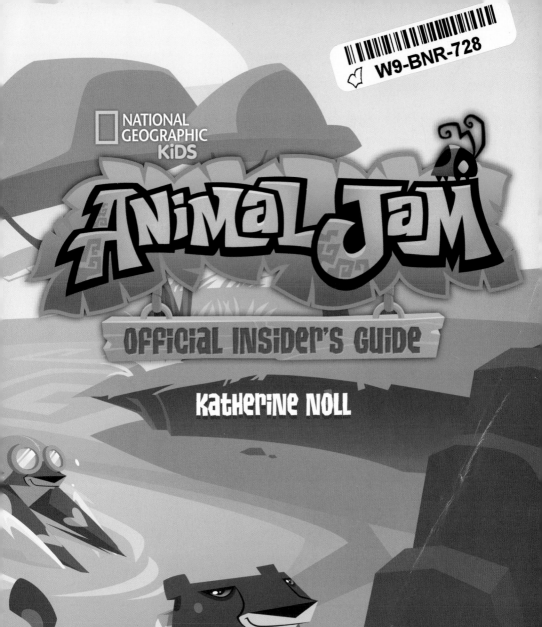

NATIONAL
GEOGRAPHIC
KiDS

ANIMAL JAM

OFFICIAL INSIDER'S GUIDE

KATHERINE NOLL

NATIONAL GEOGRAPHIC
WASHINGTON, D.C.

TABLE OF CONTENTS

WELCOME TO ANIMAL JAM!

GET READY TO PLAY WILD IN THE AMAZING ONLINE VIRTUAL PLAYGROUND OF ANIMAL JAM, CREATED ESPECIALLY FOR KIDS WHO LOVE ANIMALS.

ANIMAL JAM AND NATIONAL GEOGRAPHIC KIDS HAVE TEAMED up to bring you a fun, exciting, and safe environment to play in online, but also to inspire you to explore and protect the natural world outside your doors. In this live, multiplayer, web-based experience, you will travel to the land of Jamaa to play games, meet new friends, and explore distant lands, all while learning cool stuff about animals, plants, habitats, and more. So get ready to dig into an ancient rain forest ruin, learn what it's like to be part of a wolf pack, dive into the deepest depths of the ocean, and climb the highest mountain peak on your adventure!

This book is your guide to everything Animal Jam has to offer. You'll also get an insider's look at Jamaa and come away with tips and tricks on everything from shopping to games and even learn how Jamaa was created.

Every time you see the National Geographic yellow border you'll be provided amazing info on some of the coolest places around the world. You will soon discover that the fictional world of Jamaa isn't so different from our own planet!

So come meet over 16 million Animal Jam players, or Jammers. Welcome, and get ready for an exciting Jamaa journey.

Let Liza be your guide to Animal Jam!

Liza appears throughout this book to share her advice and tips with all Jammers. Can you find all the places she appears inside? Look closely and count every Liza you see. Then head to animaljam.com, log in to your account, and click "I have a Code." Spell out the number of Lizas you've counted (e.g., 2=two) to earn a special prize!

Jam-A-Grams   Jamaa Journal   Journey Book   Gems

Buddies   Achievements   Parties

Getting Started in Animal Jam

#1

Pick Your Animal and Name

You'll be given a set of animals to choose from—pick your favorite! Then use the spinners to create a special name for your new animal. Be creative! There are hundreds of name combinations to choose from!

#2

Fill Out Your Info

Enter your information, then create a unique username and password for your account. Ask a parent for help!

Switch Animals

Change Your Look   Actions   Chat

Username

Emotes

Want to Know More Before you Start exploring? Here is a Basic overview of what to Look for to get Started on www.aniMaLJaM.COM.

Start Your Adventure

Now you're ready to begin your adventure. Hop aboard the Blue Heron with Liza the panda Alpha, who will help you customize your look. Click on the colors, eyes, and patterns to make your animal look amazing!

Find Out More

To get updates every day in Animal Jam, check out the Jamaa Journal or the Daily Explorer, a blog about all things Animal Jam, also available at blog.animaljam.com.

Get Familiar With the Controls

You'll notice a lot of different buttons and icons on your main screen. Scroll over each to find out what they mean, and also read on to find out more!

Play Safe Online

Safety is important when doing anything on the Internet. Please check out page 230 for safety rules and to learn more about playing safe.

THE DAWN OF THE ALPHAS

TODAY THE WORLD OF JAMAA IS HOME TO MILLIONS OF ANIMALS LIVING IN PEACE. YET A LONG TIME AGO, THIS WONDERFUL WORLD WAS NEARLY LOST!

JAMAA WAS ONCE HOME TO HUNDREDS OF ANIMAL species of all shapes and sizes. These animals spent their days playing games, going to parties, building homes, and living together as friends.

Mira and Zios, the guardian spirits of Jamaa, gifted each animal species with a Heartstone, a special jewel that contained the essence of that species and held the secrets of its magic.

Read the story behind the world of **ANIMAL JAM!**

9

For many generations, all the Heartstones were kept together in a vault beneath the Lost Temple of Zios. Every animal could visit them and see the unique gifts that each species brought to Jamaa.

UNREST IN JAMAA

BUT AS TIME PASSED, THINGS CHANGED. ANIMALS began to fear and mistrust other species. Some animals stopped living together as a united community. Soon all the feelings of friendship in Jamaa were gone, and the animals built new villages for their kind only. Koalas lived and talked only with other koalas. So did rhinos. And crocodiles. Before long, all the animals in Jamaa stopped working together to make Jamaa a happy and vibrant place. Worst of all, many animal species took their Heartstones from the Lost Temple of Zios and hid them in their new villages.

It was during this time of division that the dark Phantoms first appeared.

RISE OF THE PHANTOMS

THE PHANTOMS CAME THROUGH DARK PORTALS, AND they quickly spread through the uninhabited regions of Jamaa. Wherever the Phantoms went, they left a trail of spoiling destruction. Rivers were polluted, trees became bare, and the air was thick with noxious fumes. The Phantoms consumed everything in the environment and gave nothing back. They leveled entire villages the animals had built and left the entire civilization in pieces.

LiZa

PANDA

Named after Eliza Scidmore (1856–1928), a journalist, photographer, world traveler, and the first woman to serve on the National Geographic board.

THE ALPHAS

Liza's face is a familiar one to all Jammers. She personally welcomes everyone that arrives in Jamaa and helps them get started on their adventures. Liza's always been a traveler and explorer. When she first came to Jamaa, it was a very different place. Not only were the Phantoms wreaking havoc, but also none of the animal species that lived here got along with one another. Liza's talent as a peacemaker helped bring the animals together again.

While the other Alphas travel to search for the missing Heartstones and hunt for Phantoms, Liza stays behind to guard Jamaa.

Calm and friendly, Liza is always eager to help other animals out. That is, when she's not taking photos all around Jamaa. It's her favorite thing to do!

Because animals were spread out in isolated villages, the Phantoms easily conquered these villages one by one. The animals soon discovered that if the Phantoms reached a Heartstone, they could imprison the animals of that species inside it! Each time the Phantoms captured a Heartstone, an entire species disappeared from Jamaa.

Mira and Zios watched in horror as the Phantoms spread throughout Jamaa. As guardian spirits, it hurt them to see the land they loved become corrupted, and they knew they could bring Jamaa back to life if the Phantoms were repelled. In time, they could make the skies and waters clear again, and if they could recover the lost Heartstones, thousands of animals could return to Jamaa. As time drew on, however, the Phantom threat grew only more fearsome and unstoppable.

Taking a Stand

REMEMBERING HOW MUCH THEY HAD ACCOMPLISHED when they lived and worked together, the remaining six species gathered their Heartstones, left their villages, and returned to the Lost Temple of Zios. As the tigers, monkeys, koalas, pandas, rabbits, and wolves of Jamaa gathered together for one last stand against the Phantoms, Mira and Zios saw that it would not be enough.

In desperation, the guardian spirits of Jamaa searched other lands for six leaders who could

THE ALPHAS

GRAHAM
MONKEY

Named after Alexander Graham Bell (1847–1922), inventor of the telephone and second president of the National Geographic Society.

Graham thinks the other Alphas always do things the hard way. For example, Liza once tracked the giraffe Heartstone to a Phantom cavern sealed by an enormous boulder. By the time Graham got there, Liza had dozens of animals straining to move the stone, but it wouldn't budge.

For Graham, it was the simplest thing in the world to build a waterwheel using a system of gears, pulleys, and counterweights. With the pull of a lever, the gigantic rock moved with ease! Broken gadgets and gizmos are quickly fixed when Graham handles them. Is it magic, science, or simply extraordinary luck? The other Alphas aren't sure, but they like the amazing results Graham achieves.

Before Cosmo came to Jamaa, he seemed to be a fairly typical koala: He spent most of his time in trees, eating leaves and napping. But even then, there was always something different about Cosmo. The koala understands plants in a very special way.

Cosmo knows what plants are saying—to each other, to animals, and sometimes even to themselves. The plants in Jamaa talk to Cosmo and tell him how to create potions with hundreds of uses.

As the youngest of the Alphas, Cosmo and Peck are always joking around. But there's one thing Cosmo never jokes about. He has a deep respect for the power of the natural world, perhaps because he is able to communicate with so much of it.

COSMO

KOALA

Named after the Cosmos Club, a private club in Washington, D.C., where the first ever meeting of the National Geographic Society took place in 1888.

wield the power of their entire species. They even looked to our world, and it was here that they found six extraordinary animals and brought them to Jamaa: Sir Gilbert the regal tiger, Cosmo the knowledge-able koala, Graham the inventive monkey, Greely the mysterious wolf, Liza the curious panda, and Peck the creative rabbit. These were six remarkable animals with different personalities, but they were united in their strength of character and their respect for the natural world.

Mira and Zios chose well, and these very different animals soon formed a family.

To help in the battle against the Phantoms, Mira and Zios gave the new leaders Alpha Stones, six special jewels that focused the strength and abilities of their entire species. With these stones, the six chosen animals became Alphas, the heroes chosen to save Jamaa in its darkest hour!

The Alphas set about making a plan that utilized each of their unique abilities to defeat the Phantoms. Once the plan was finalized, they joined the rest of the animals who had gathered together to face the flood of Phantoms before them. When the animals saw the magnificent Alphas, they felt their own bravery return. The Alphas felt the strength of the Alpha Stones flowing through them, and with many roars, howls, and cheers, they all stormed into battle.

THE FIGHT TO SAVE JAMAA

THE BATTLE FOR JAMAA WAS EPIC, WITH THE ANIMALS and Alphas fighting not just for themselves, but also for the beautiful land that Jamaa once was. Animals that were once scared of the Phantoms found new courage, and animals that had shunned and despised others worked side by side with different species.

As the animals marched forward, the Phantoms escaped by fleeing into their dark portals. But just as the last of the Phantoms were retreating, they overtook Zios and vanished with him into a portal. Mira quickly dove into a dark portal, following Zios and the Phantoms, disappearing as the portal closed.

The sudden absence of Zios and Mira was a tragic blow to the animals, yet despite their sadness, they realized that for the first time many of them could remember, Jamaa was free of the Phantoms!

THE ALPHAS

Solitary by nature and a master of stealth, Greely spends most of his time alone and far from Jamaa, observing the movements of the Phantoms and sabotaging them from the shadows. These movements make many animals very nervous; it sometimes seems as though Greely can appear anywhere, anytime.

Some of the other Alphas don't trust Greely and his methods, but they certainly respect him. He knows more about the Phantoms and their movements than anyone, and it's possible the Phantoms fear him more than any of the other Alphas.

Greely

WOLF

Named after Adolphus Greely (1844–1935), Arctic explorer and a founding member of the National Geographic Society.

Rebuilding Their Home

JAMAA HAD BEEN SAVED, BUT THE DAMAGE THE Phantoms had caused was everywhere. Plants and trees were sick, clouds of poison smoke hung in the air, and the land itself was littered with burnt plastic refuse that seemed to follow the Phantoms wherever they went. The Alphas knew it would be the responsibility of every animal in Jamaa, including themselves, to return the land to its former glory.

While the animals worked hard to rebuild, cleansing power from the Alpha Stones flowed through the Alphas and into the land. Soon, the rivers were running clear, the trees regained their leaves, and the air was fresh and crisp. The pristine beauty of Jamaa had spread from the top of Mt. Shiveer to the bottom of Deep Blue.

During this time, Liza stayed in Jamaa Township to protect the village and help new animals that came to Jamaa, while the other Alphas separated to explore lost lands and track the Phantoms to their source. They were able to restore many of the lands that had been taken over by the Phantoms, and many Heartstones were returned. Animals trapped inside the Heartstones were freed to return to their homes, and they were welcomed by all their animal friends. In a short time, the world of Jamaa began to resemble the beautiful world it once was.

THE ALPHAS

Peck is noisy and excitable, but Mira also sees a creative problem-solver in her. In Jamaa, Peck is a musician and a talented artist who has done much to beautify the world. She inspires all the animals in Jamaa to explore their creative side and join her in art projects.

Have you ever had a friend who seemed to be made out of pure energy, who could never sit still, and who was always trying to involve you in some new, crazy scheme of theirs? That's Peck! She moves in a blur, gets bored easily, and never seems to run out of ideas. She takes her role as a mentor to other animals very seriously, though, and she is determined to get Jamaa's animals into shape and ready for whatever the Phantoms might throw at them.

Peck
RABBIT

Named after Annie Smith Peck (1850–1935), a record-setting mountain climber and explorer.

THE ALPHAS

Ever since he was a cub, Sir Gilbert wondered what it must be like to be a monkey. Or a giraffe. Or a penguin, shark, or rabbit. All other animals fascinate him!

Sir Gilbert's favorite thing about living in Jamaa is socializing with many different kinds of animals. He's impeccably polite, quietly dignified, and sensibly cautious. Sometimes the other Alphas tease Sir Gilbert about his regal manners, but everyone looks to the noble tiger as a leader.

SiR GiLBeRT
TIGER

Named after Gilbert H. Grosvenor (1875–1966), a writer and geographer who not only became the first full-time editor of National Geographic magazine but served as president of the National Geographic Society, too.

A LastiNG Peace?

MILLIONS OF ANIMALS NOW LIVE IN PEACE AND happiness in Jamaa. The Alphas continue to explore new lands, and whenever they are able to drive the Phantoms out of an area or reclaim a Heartstone, the animals of Jamaa celebrate that they have new lands to play in and new animal friends to play with!

Many years have passed since all of Jamaa was nearly lost, but now some of the Phantoms have returned, and they are once again trying to ruin the peace and joy of Jamaa.

Read on to find out the best tips and tricks to help the animals of Jamaa rid their land of Phantoms forever!

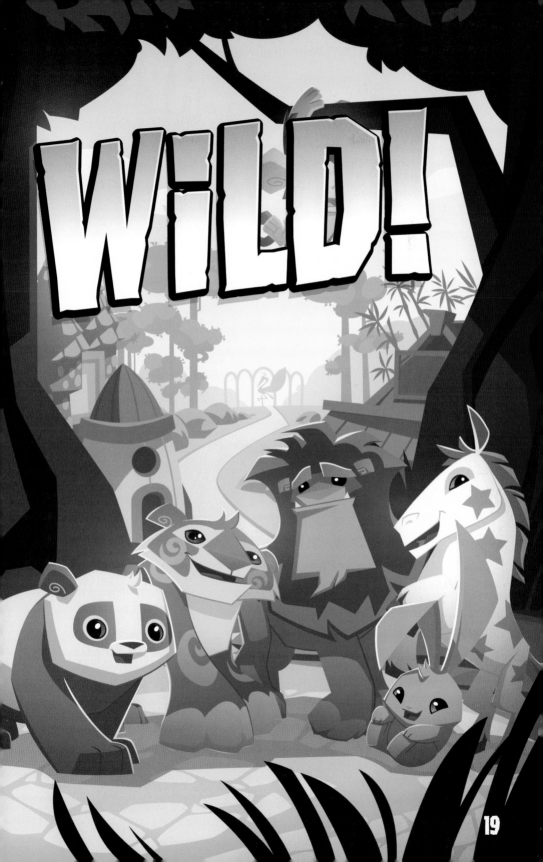

EXPLORE

FUN FACT

JAMAA HAS ONLY ONE OCEAN, JUST LIKE EARTH. ALMOST THREE-FOURTHS OF EARTH IS COVERED BY ONE BIG OCEAN. PARTS OF THIS OCEAN HAVE BEEN GIVEN NAMES: ATLANTIC OCEAN, ARCTIC OCEAN, INDIAN OCEAN, AND PACIFIC OCEAN.

Mt. Shiveer

Jamaa Township

Appondale

Kimbara Outback

World Map

IF YOU'RE LOOKING TO explore Jamaa, all you need to do is decide where you want to go and click that area of the map! It's that easy. You'll find the World Map on the bottom right-hand corner of the screen. Each land in Jamaa is full of fantastic facts, fun games, and interesting sites to see and play in.

You can also highlight areas that have theaters and clothing, furniture, and pet shops by using the icons on the right side of your screen.

If you want to go exploring and brave the wilds without a map, you can walk or swim from place to place. To delve into the oceans, you'll need an ocean animal. Look for the wave icon on the "Choose an Animal" menu for an animal that can help you explore the ocean depths.

JaMaa!

SarePia Forest

CoraL Canyons

Lost TempLe of Zios

CrystaL Sands

Bahari Bay

Kani Cove

Deep Blue

CrystaL Reef

BECOME YOUR FAVORITE ANIMAL!

IN JAMAA, YOU CAN PLAY AS YOUR FAVORITE ANIMAL—BUT THAT'S NOT ALL!

YOU CAN ALSO CUSTOMIZE YOUR ANIMAL WITH DIFFERENT COLORS, EYES, PATTERNS, AND clothing, making a creature that's totally unique and yours alone.

From time to time, you'll notice some of the animal species in Jamaa are traveling or exploring, which means you cannot choose them when making a new animal. In the wild, animals travel for lots of different reasons. Sometimes they are searching for food, looking for warmer weather, or just hoping for a change of scenery! Just like wild animals, the species in Jamaa will sometimes decide to go traveling or exploring, too. Usually they come back. You'll just have to wait and see if they return to Jamaa! Check out all the animals living in Jamaa as of now. Since the Alphas are always searching for lost Heartstones, new species are discovered all the time!

Bunny

As a bunny, you'll be the hoppiest animal in Jamaa!

A rabbit has almost twice as many taste buds on its tongue as a human does. *Turn to page 58 to learn more about bunnies.*

Cheetah

Zoom around Jamaa as the fastest land animal in the world.

Cheetah cubs have a mane on their neck and shoulders that looks like a mini-mohawk! *Turn to page 84 to learn more about cheetahs.*

Crocodile

Everyone will wonder what you're smiling about.

When a croc sits with its mouth wide open revealing its sharp teeth, it's not trying to be scary. That's how it sweats! *Turn to page 148 to learn more about crocodiles.*

Deer

Leap around Sarepia Forest as a graceful deer.

The largest member of the deer species is the moose. *Turn to page 104 to learn more about deer.*

Dolphin

Flip for joy in Bahari Bay as a dolphin.

Dolphins can swim up to five times faster than the fastest swimming human and dive as deep as 2,000 feet (610 m). *Turn to page 132 to learn more about dolphins.*

Eagle

Get a bird's-eye view of all of Jamaa as you soar high above.

It's tough for eagles to super-size their dinner. This carnivorous bird can lift only about half of its body weight! *Turn to page 190 to learn more about eagles.*

Elephant

As an elephant, you'll never forget all the cool things there are to do in Jamaa!

One elephant can eat 300 pounds (136 kg) of food in one day! *Turn to page 88 to learn more about elephants.*

Fox

As a quick fox you can jump over any lazy animals who might be in your way!

In legends and fairy tales, foxes are often described as cunning, magical creatures. *Turn to page 119 to learn more about foxes.*

Giraffe

Reach new heights in Appondale as a giraffe.

You might sleep with your head on a comfy pillow, but the giraffe almost always sleeps standing up! *Turn to page 91 to learn more about giraffes.*

Horse

Race to the finish line in the Jamaa Derby as a horse.

Surround sound! Because they can rotate their ears 180 degrees, horses have excellent hearing. *Turn to page 123 to learn more about horses.*

Kangaroo

If you're feeling jumpy, go explore Kimbara Outback as a kangaroo.

More kangaroos than people live in Australia. *Turn to page 207 to learn more about kangaroos.*

Koala

Explore Jamaa as a cute and cuddly koala.

Koalas don't need to worry about bad breath. Their diet of eucalyptus leaves makes them smell like minty cough drops! *Turn to page 206 to learn more about koalas.*

Lion

You'll be the King or Queen of Jamaa as this royal cat.

A lion pride can be as few as 3 animals or as many as 30. *Turn to page 122 to learn more about lions.*

Monkey

If you want to monkey around, this is the animal for you.

They got their name for a reason. A group of howler monkeys can be heard up to 3 miles (5 km) away! *Turn to page 77 to learn more about monkeys.*

Octopus

You'll always have an extra helping hand if you pick this ocean animal.

If an octopus loses one of its eight arms, a new one grows back in its place! *Turn to page 180 to learn more about octopuses.*

Panda

What's black and white and adorable all over? A panda, of course!

Pandas spend most of their day eating—and going to the bathroom. Now that's one pet you wouldn't want to clean up after! *Turn to page 61 to learn more about pandas.*

Penguin

Put a little waddle in your walk as a penguin.

Every penguin has its own unique voice, which helps it to find its mate or chick in a crowd. *Turn to page 133 to learn more about penguins.*

Raccoon

Only you will know what you're really thinking behind that mask!

High five! The tracks of a raccoon are easy to identify: Its front paws have five toes, and the tracks look a lot like small human hands. *Turn to page 105 to learn more about raccoons.*

Rhino

As a rhino you can charge right into the middle of all the action in Jamaa Township.

Adult rhinos have no natural predators except for humans. *Turn to page 89 to learn more about rhinos.*

Sea Turtle

Strap on a shell and explore the sea!

The shell on the back of a turtle is called the carapace, while the covering on a turtle's belly is called a plastron. *Turn to page 158 to learn more about sea turtles.*

Seal

Slippery seals glide gracefully under the waves!

Elephant seals can dive 5,000 feet (1,500 m) deep into the ocean and spend up to two hours at that depth. *Turn to page 138 to learn more about seals.*

Shark

My, what big teeth you have!

Instead of bone, a shark's skeleton is made mostly of cartilage— the material your nose and ears are made of. *Turn to page 170 to learn more about sharks.*

Snow Leopard

Ward off the chill in snowy Mt. Shiveer with a built-in fur coat!

Their strong legs enable snow leopards to leap as far as 50 feet (15 m) in one bound! *Turn to page 194 to learn more about snow leopards.*

Tiger

Sport some stylish stripes as a tiger.

Snack attack! Tigers don't eat only large prey animals like buffalo and deer. They'll also gobble up turtles and frogs. *Turn to page 70 to learn more about tigers.*

Wolf and Arctic Wolf

Have a howling good time playing Animal Jam as a wolf!

Little Red Riding Hood got it wrong! Wolves almost never attack humans. The idea of the big bad wolf is a total fairy tale. *Turn to page 100 to learn more about wolves.*

Certain animals are available for Jammers who have purchased an **ANIMAL JAM CLUB MEMBERSHIP.** Once in a while, members-only animals are made available to all Jammers, so check often!

ANIMAL DENS

GINGERBREAD HOUSE

PRINCESS CASTLE

WHETHER IT'S A GINGERBREAD HOUSE, A CASTLE, OR A VOLCANO, THERE'S NO PLACE LIKE HOME!

HOME IN ANIMAL JAM IS A DEN, BUT EACH den is as unique and different as the player who owns it. Animal Jam players get to show their personalities through their den décor. Always wanted to live underwater in a sunken ship? Or have a house filled with plushies? You can in Jamaa.

Den Sweet Den: Every player starts off with the cozy Small House den, and there are lots of additional dens to choose from.

Amazing Animal Architects

SO YOU THINK YOUR DECKED-OUT DEN IS pretty awesome? Wait until you see what these animals build in the wild!

Busy Beaver Builders

Beavers use their strong teeth and jaws to build their homes, called lodges, in large ponds.

Insect Skyscraper

In Africa, termites build their mounds up to 30 feet (9 m) high and they contain gardens, food storage areas, and cooling and ventilation systems!

Bowerbirds That Beautify!

Bowerbirds of New Guinea and Australia decorate their nests with everything from paint made from their own spit, seashells, and even garlands made from caterpillar poop!

Personalize Your Den

If you're in a land den, you can shop for your den in the Jam Mart Furniture catalog. If you're in an ocean den, you'll see the Sunken Treasures catalog. You can pick out furniture, floors, walls, toys, accessories, and more. Create a cool theme or pick out the items you like best — it's your choice.

ALPHA TIP

Liza

You can find mysterious items for your den in the Chamber of Knowledge in the Lost Temple of Zios. Make sure to go all the way to the third floor to find the Mystery Emporium.

SPARKLING
DIAMONDS & GEMS

THERE ARE LOTS OF COOL THINGS TO BUY IN JAMAA —EVERYTHING FROM CLOTHES, ACCESSORIES, FURNITURE, PETS, DENS, AND MORE!

Gems

The currency in Jamaa is colorful, sparkly Gems. There are many different ways to earn Gems, and they're all fun! Playing your favorite Animal Jam games will earn you Gems. The better you are at the game, and the more you play, the more Gems you'll earn. You can also recycle any unwanted clothing, accessories, or den items for Gems. Before you do, make certain you don't want those items anymore.

Diamonds

Jammers can also get some of the coolest and rarest items at the Diamond Shop in Jamaa Township! Just like Gems, Diamonds can be used to buy awesome items. The inventory at the Diamond Shop contains amazing animals, rare pets, and epic items.

Liza

ALPHA TIP

Once a day you can play the Daily Spin. Spin the wheel that pops up when you log in to win Gems. Jammers can win anywhere from 25 to 500 Gems, as well as Diamonds. If you log in every day, you might be lucky enough to earn double or even triple Gems and Diamonds. That could add up to 1,500 Gems or 3 Diamonds a day!

DIAMONDS ARE OLD. And when we say old, we're not kidding around. Diamonds found in kimberlite deposits were formed up to 3.3 billion years ago in the Earth's mantle. Kimberlite pipes, created by magma, connect the Earth's crust to the mantle. They carry diamonds and other rocks and minerals to the surface.

Most of the Earth's natural diamond

Real Diamonds That Shine!

deposits are found in Africa, although the Golconda region in India is home to one of the oldest diamond mine areas in the world. Diamonds vary in color from black to colorless. The colorless or pale blue stones are the most valued but are also the rarest. The hardness, brilliance, and sparkle of diamonds are what make them so desirable. In fact, the sparkly gem is the hardest natural substance on Earth.

The Archduke Joseph

This 76.02-carat diamond sold for nearly $21.5 million in 2012, making it one of the most expensive colorless diamonds ever sold at auction! The cushion-shaped diamond once belonged to Archduke Joseph August of Austria, for whom the gem is named.

The Centenary Diamond

A jeweler cuts a diamond to give it that brilliant sparkle it's known for. When the Centenary diamond was first mined in 1986, it weighed 599.10 carats. It took almost three years to transform it into one of the world's largest modern-cut and flawless diamonds. It's now a trim (but sparkly) 273.85 carats.

Mountain of Light

The Mountain of Light, or Koh-i-noor, diamond is mounted into the Imperial British State Crown. It dates back to 1304 and is said to be cursed! Stories say any male ruler who wears the 105.60-carat diamond will pay with his life. No wonder queens were the only British monarchs who dared to wear it!

The Hope Diamond

Throughout history, people have been willing to cheat, lie, and even kill to get their hands on diamonds. The blue Hope diamond is no different, with a past that includes theft, financial disaster, catastrophe, and death. But it sure is pretty!

The Great Star of Africa

The largest cut diamond in the world at 530.20 carats, the Cullinan I, or Star of Africa, diamond was cut from a 3,106-carat rough diamond in 1908. The fabulous diamond was mounted into the British Sovereign's Royal Sceptre. Today it's on display in the Tower of London in England.

AWESOME ADVENTURES!

ANIMAL JAM NEEDS YOUR HELP!

THE PHANTOMS HAVE RETURNED and are threatening the peace of Jamaa. If you are brave, clever, and wild, you can join with the Alphas and save this world!

Help stop the Phantoms by going to the Lost Temple of Zios. Here you'll find an entrance to the Adventure Base Camp. If this is your first Adventure, make sure to visit the Training Grounds. Liza, the panda Alpha, will teach you the tips and tricks she has learned in the wild, including how to outsmart and defeat the Phantoms.

Once Liza has trained you, head to a portal to choose your Adventure. There are two modes: Normal and Hard. It might be a good idea to practice in Normal mode before tackling the Adventure in Hard mode. Some Adventures can be played with up to four Jammers. Get your best buddies together to form a dream team of Adventurers! With each Adventure you complete, your courage level will increase. The more courageous you are, the easier it will be to level up!

There are lots of cool Adventures you can play! Do them by yourself or with a friend.

Return of the Phantoms

The Phantoms have returned and Bunny Burrow is in trouble! Nasty Phantom Pipes have polluted rivers and plants that the bunnies need for a healthy home. Help Liza clean up the rivers, rescue all the bunnies, and defeat any Phantoms you encounter along the way.

#1

GRAHAM

ALPHA TIP

Adventures are filled with hidden paths that can lead to hidden treasure! There's no telling how much treasure is out there, so keep your eyes peeled. Secret passages can also be found in Adventures, but they can only be used by certain animals. If you find one of these secret passages and aren't playing as the right animal, don't worry. You can play Adventures over and over again as all of your animals!

The Phantom Portal

The Phantoms have opened a portal to Jamaa and have discovered how to wilt chomper plants! Find a way to revive the plants, and help Liza close the portal. Teamwork will help you work through this Adventure.

#2

#3

Meet Cosmo

Cosmo, the koala Alpha, needs help creating a new seed that will help defeat the Phantoms. Explore the surrounding area to find the ingredients that Cosmo needs, but watch out for Phantom Sprouters—they make more Phantoms!

#4

The Hive

Explore the dark Phantom Hive to find the Phantom King. Make sure to bring a light! You'll meet Greely, the wolf Alpha, as you make your way through. But be on your guard—you'll need to be clever to take on the Phantom King!

#5

The Great Escape

Dark sludge has started to rain down on Jamaa. Cosmo thinks it may be coming from the eerie Phantom Tower, a place that was originally built by the Alphas, but is now a Phantom dungeon! To find out what the Phantoms are planning you'll have to willingly let the Phantoms capture you. Will you make it out? Only the bravest Jammers will be able to unlock the secrets of the Tower and escape!

#6

Greely's Inferno

Jamaa's volcano is about to erupt! Can you help stop it? Head to the top to find Graham, the monkey Alpha, who will help you make your way through the volcano. You'll also meet Greely and discover his secret lair inside. But smoking hot lava isn't all you'll have to face. With puzzles to solve and Phantoms to defeat, this Adventure promises to be a tough challenge!

Real-Life Adventurers

IS A LIFE OF ADVENTURE AND EXCITEMENT CALLING YOU? THROUGHOUT history, some people have been daring trailblazers, going places and doing things no one had ever done before. Learn about some of these adventurers and see what they inspire YOU to do!

Sir Ernest Henry Shackleton

His dad wanted him to be a doctor, but Irish-born Ernest Shackleton wanted a life of adventure! In 1890, at the age of 16, he joined the British Navy and eventually became a polar explorer who went on three expeditions to the Antarctic. He climbed Mount Erebus and made many valuable scientific discoveries in this vastly unexplored land. On one of Shackleton's later journeys, his ship got stuck in the ice and he and his crew had to live on floating ice for months!

Bessie Coleman

Born in 1892 Coleman, an African American, dreamed of becoming a pilot. When flying schools in the United States refused her admittance, the persistent Coleman refused to take no for an answer and went to France to learn. There she became the world's first black woman to earn a pilot's license. No leisurely flights in the sky for the daring Coleman! She specialized in stunt flying, parachuting, and aerial tricks.

Neil Armstrong

On July 20, 1969, Neil Armstrong did what no other person had done before and what many believed wasn't even possible: He set foot on the moon! Armstrong knew from a young age that he wanted to be a pilot. In 1962, he joined the National Aeronautics and Space Administration's (NASA) space program and began work on the ultimate adventure: space travel. Armstrong has said that the most thrilling part of the moon mission was not his steps on the moon, but the tricky landing on the lunar surface!

And of Course We Can't Forget . . .

Animal Jam's own National Geographic Explorers and scientists, Brady Barr and Tierney Thys! They've spent their careers protecting and studying our environment and the amazing animals that live in it. These adventurers crawl with crocodiles and explore the ocean depths, then come back to Jamaa to share with us all they've learned.

ACHIEVEMENT!

25

100,000

250

50

over ACHIEVERS

Get rewarded for your awesome accomplishments in Animal Jam!

YOU'RE PLAYING A GAME IN JAMAA WHEN ALL OF A SUDDEN YOU HEAR fireworks as a pop-up message flashes on the screen. You've earned an Achievement! These fun messages are a way of celebrating your Animal Jam accomplishments. You earn Achievements simply by exploring, playing games, or shopping.

For instance, you can earn an Achievement after you have played Best Dressed five times, or when you have purchased 25 clothing items, or for the first time you change your colors! Keep exploring and look for all the ways you can earn Achievements in Jamaa.

ALPHA TIP

COSMO

Jammers can earn plaques from Animal Jam HQ (AJHQ) by winning contests, having their art and howls featured in Jammer Central, being featured on the Epic Dens list, and more!

Amazing Animal Achievers

SAVING LIVES? TRAVELING THE WORLD? IT'S NO PROBLEM FOR THESE AWESOME real-life animals who have achieved some truly remarkable things!

Superdog saves cats!

Most dogs like to chase or bark at cats, but not Wuffy! This kindhearted pooch has dedicated her life to rescuing cats in trouble. The first time Wuffy saved the day was when she found four sick kittens. She nursed them back to health, much to her owner's surprise! Since then, Wuffy has rescued more than 200 cats and even got a job with a local rescue group as a foster mom to cats in need.

Penguin is knighted!

It's certainly an achievement to be knighted by the Norwegian King's Guard, and it's an honor that Sir Nils Olav, the king penguin, has experienced firsthand. The Guard, who protect Norway's royal family, have been adopting king penguins as mascots because the birds' black-and-white feathers resemble the soldiers' uniforms.

Dog saves owner's life!

When Debbie Parkhurst choked on a piece of apple, her dog Tony inexplicably seemed to know exactly what to do. The golden retriever pushed Debbie to the ground and began bouncing on her chest, similar to movements used in the Heimlich maneuver. The dog's efforts dislodged the piece of apple from Debbie's windpipe and prevented her from choking!

Globe-trotting dog sees the sites!

Oscar the terrier mix has seen the Sphinx in Egypt, zip-lined in Costa Rica, ridden a camel in India, and visited the Eiffel Tower in Paris, France. He's also been on safari in Africa and had his picture taken at the Colosseum in Rome, Italy! The mild-mannered dog is a great traveler and together with his owner, Joanne Lefson, has traveled about 46,000 miles (74,030 km)! Lefson takes Oscar all over the world to prove that shelter dogs make fantastic pets.

JOURNEY BOOK

FILL YOUR JOURNEY BOOK AS YOU TRAVEL THROUGH JAMAA AND WIN PRIZES!

YOU'LL NOTICE THAT EACH land and ocean in Jamaa is home to different animals and plants. You might spot a platypus in Kimbara Outback, a rattlesnake in Coral Canyons, a hammerhead shark in Kani Cove, or a family of skunks in Sarepia Forest! When you see an animal or plant native to the land you're in, click on it. Not only will you learn awesome facts about the species, but you can add it to your Journey Book, too.

They are not all easy to find. Each land and ocean in Jamaa has its own page in the Journey Book, which is the book button on the top left of your screen. Try to match the outlines in your book to the plants and animals you see around Jamaa.

In the Field

SCIENTISTS, BIRD-WATCHERS, ARTISTS, and even casual nature lovers keep records of animals and plants they see in the wild. If you love searching for wildlife for your Animal Jam Journey Book, you might also enjoy keeping a journal of flora and fauna you find on vacation, at a nearby park, or in your very own backyard. All you need is a notebook and a pen or pencil. When you spot a plant, animal, or bird you want to add to your book, write down where you saw it, the date, what the weather was like, and a detailed description. Draw a picture and you'll have a great record of your real-life nature adventures.

John James Audubon

BORN IN 1785, John James Audubon was a French-American artist, ornithologist, and naturalist who traveled the American wilderness to draw birds, animals, and plants in their natural habitats.

His life-size bird portraits and descriptions of wilderness life were first published in 1827. A huge success, Audubon's works paved the way for bird-watching to become a popular pastime in the late 1800s. It's a hobby that millions of people enjoy around the world to this day!

Named for John James Audubon, the National Audubon Society was founded in 1905. The society works to protect and conserve birds and other wildlife along with the natural ecosystems they live in.

The animals move, so sometimes you have to wait quietly until they show themselves. They might be swimming, hanging out on rocks, playing high in the treetops, or far off in the distance. Plants can blend into their surroundings so keep a lookout! Certain parties, like the Paradise Party, also give you the opportunity to add to your Journey Book.

The Journey Book is a fun way to learn about the animals, plants, and ecosystems. Once you've found all the plants and animals in a land, you'll be rewarded with a rare and awesome prize!

PECK

ALPHA TIP

The clownfish in Crystal Reef can be hard to find. Here's a hint: These cute fish live (and hide) in sea anemones.

parties

A DAY DOESN'T GO BY WHEN THERE ISN'T SOMETHING TO CELEBRATE IN JAMAA! JOIN IN AND WHOOP IT UP WILD.

Animals Get Social

IN THE WILD, IT'S NOT ALWAYS every animal for itself. Animals such as wolves and dolphins have complex social lives. They'd be right at home at a party in Jamaa!

Wolves live, hunt, raise their young, and protect their territory together in packs, and dolphins do the same in family groups called pods. Communication skills are very important to their survival, which makes being social a necessity. A misunderstanding could mean a missed meal or a young pup or calf left unprotected!

Wolves communicate with each other by whimpering, howling, barking, and

Gray wolves

whining. Bottlenose dolphins are very vocal and squeak, whistle, grunt, and moan to converse.

Wolves and dolphins might not blow up balloons and eat cake to celebrate, but both of these animals know how to have fun. Playing is an important part of their lives. It teaches the animals how to work together, and it hones skills used in hunting.

My Parties

ADVENTURES

Wolves Only Party
In 44 minutes

Horses Only Party
In 44 minutes

Paradise Party
In 44 minutes

LEARN ALL ABOUT THE LATEST PARTIES happening in Jamaa by clicking on the party icon in the top left corner of the screen. You'll see a list of the parties planned for the day and how long it will be until they start. If a party is currently taking place, there's no wait—you can join in on the fun right away!

There's also another great reason to get festive—parties also allow you to buy cool party-themed items for your den, including exclusive den music and clothing.

Parties last for 30 minutes and the next one starts right after, so you'll never have to wait long to join the latest bash. Life's one big party in Jamaa!

Happy Jamaalidays!

THROUGHOUT THE YEAR, HOLIDAYS are celebrated in Jamaa. Favorite among Jammers are the Jamaalidays, a series of celebrations held in the winter. Most Jammers catch the spirit of giving and give gifts to each other! Mark your calendar! Other fun festivals include:

Friendship Festival (February)
Good buddies make Jamaa the special place that it is, so all Jammers celebrate their appreciation of friendship during this time.

Lucky Day (March)
Break out your green gear and celebrate all the lucky things in your life! If you explore Jamaa during this festival, a little extra luck might fall your way.

Freedom Day (July)
Dress up in red, white, and blue, and check out the Jamaa fireworks show!

Night of the Phantoms (October)
Jammers dress up in silly and scary costumes to trick the Phantoms and prevent them from causing mischief.

Feast of Thanks (November)
Take some time to celebrate what you're thankful for with other Jammers.

ALPHA TIP

COSMO

Gems and Diamonds aren't the only things that glitter in Jamaa! Each month in Epic Wonders, a dazzling birthstone is for sale.

JAM-A-GRAMS

JAMAA HAS ITS VERY OWN MAIL SYSTEM!

SEND MESSAGES TO YOUR BUDDIES WITH JAM-A-GRAMS, FUN POSTCARDS YOU can customize. Jam-A-Grams come in different themes to celebrate whatever might be happening in Jamaa. Celebrate the seasons, share your favorite animal or land in Jamaa, let buddies know you like their den or costumes, or even wish someone a happy birthday with a Jam-A-Gram.

Look for the mail icon at the top left corner of your screen to get started. You can read Jam-A-Grams others have sent to you and reply to them here, too. Members can attach a gift to their Jam-A-Gram. Don't send anything you don't want to lose!

Can someone help me?
I can help you!
This is so cool!
Animal Jam rocks!
Oceans are awesome!
Pets are cool!
Let's go to...
Party in...
Let's shop at...
Let's play...
Hello!
Thanks!
Yes.
Let's be buddies!
Do you want to trade?
Winter is here!

Hi!
Hi everyone!
Hey everybody!
Yo!
Hiya!
What's up Jammers?
What's going on?
Goodbye!
I have to go!
So long Jammers.
Bye everybody!
See you later!
I'm out of here.
Bye bye!

CHATTER MOUTHS

IN ADDITION TO JAM-A-GRAMS, YOU CAN TALK to other Jammers who are currently on your screen using the chat feature. There are three different kinds of chat options for all Jammers:

Restricted Chat allows you to type from a pre-selected dictionary of words. All new accounts start with this type of chat.

Bubble Chat lets you see other Jammers' chat and reply using prewritten messages, but you cannot type.

Safe (Free) Chat allows you to type words not in the preselected dictionary. This option must be turned on by your parents in the Parent Dashboard. Safe Chat is a members-only feature.

Hello!

SWEET MUSIC

HOW LOW CAN YOU GO?

HORSEPLAY

BUNNIES

Best Friends!

Chatting in the Wild

WHAT'S AN ANIMAL TO DO WHEN IT wants to send a message? In the wild, animals don't use Jam-A-Grams or chat bars. Instead, animals communicate with sight, sound, and touch, just like humans do. Some animals release chemicals called pheromones into the air to relay information. This chemical communication can be used to mark territory, attract mates, identify other animals, and to find prey and food.

Kangaroos

Kangaroos will thump the ground with their powerful hind legs to warn other kangaroos of impending danger.

Fiddler Crabs

Hey, how ya doing? It's hard to miss it when this crab waves! To attract females, the male fiddler crab waves his oversize claw in the air before tapping it on the ground.

Cats

Cats rub faces with others or against a person's leg to transfer scents from its facial glands. It's how the cat claims objects, other animals, and even people as part of its territory. When a cat does this to you, it's not saying "I like you," but "You're mine!"

Elephants

Elephants touch and smell each other with their trunks to form and maintain close relationships.

EMOtes

IF YOU'RE HAPPY AND YOU KNOW IT USE AN EMOTE!

OR EVEN IF YOU'RE FEELING ANGRY, sad, surprised, or confused. Jammers can express a world of emotions by clicking on the Emotes button in their toolbar. It's an easy way to let everyone know exactly how you're feeling.

MEMBERS ONLY

Animal Emotions

CAN AN ELEPHANT GRIEVE? A DOG LAUGH? STUDYING EMOTIONS IN ANIMALS IS difficult because humans are known to project their own feelings onto animals. This is called anthropomorphism. Yet research and observation have led scientists to believe that certain animals are capable of grief, love, joy, and happiness much like humans.

Elephant Tears

When an elephant is reunited with family members, what look like tears will flow down its face. This fluid comes from the elephant's temporal glands, which are between the ear and eye. When passing the place a friend or family member has died, elephants will stop for a moment to quietly stand, sometimes touching the elephant's bones.

Laughing Dogs

If you've ever seen dogs at play, you know that pooches know how to have fun! But did you know that they have their own canine laugh, too? Researchers recorded dogs playing in a park and picked up on a breathy noise that was different from normal panting. When the noise was played for other dogs, they began to play! Canine laughter must be contagious.

Sympathetic Rats

To test how helpful rats could be, one rat was placed in a cage. Another rat was allowed to move freely around it. The free rat spent a lot of time trying to open the door to help the other rat escape. At one point in the experiment the rat had a choice: to free the caged rat or snack on chocolate chips. The kind rat freed the captive first before eating—and it even shared its snack!

and ACTIONS

THAT'S NOT ALL YOU CAN DO TO EXPRESS YOURSELF!

DANCE, HOP, SLEEP, SIT, AND PLAY BY clicking on the Actions button. Dancing foxes, hopping penguins, snoozing crocodiles, and playful elephants are all common sights in Jamaa. All the animals in Jamaa are unique and their actions reflect that. Try dancing and playing when using different animals. Each animal has its own style!

THERE'S A LOT TO JUMP FOR JOY ABOUT IN JAMAA!

Hop

PLEASE DON'T "PAWS" THE MUSIC!

Dance

Play

GET READY. SET. GO! LET'S PLAY WILD IN JAMAA!

HAVING SO MUCH FUN IS EXHAUSTING. TIME FOR SOME SWEET DREAMS.

Sleep

ALPHA TIP

SIR GILBERT

There's always time to play in Jamaa! Ocean animals have a different set of Actions to choose from. They can dive, swirl, pose, play, and dance.

BUDDIES

FIND YOUR FRIENDS ANYTIME, ANYWHERE, BY PUTTING THEM ON YOUR BUDDY LIST.

JAMAA IS A BIG PLACE WITH LOTS going on. Keep track of your buddies with the buddy list. Look for the buddies icon at the top left corner of your screen.

Each Jammer can have up to 100 buddies on their list. If your list gets full, you can turn off buddy requests by going to the icon that looks like a gear in the top right corner of your screen. You can also remove buddies from your list at any time. Be careful! Once they're removed, you'll have to find them again if you want to re-add that Jammer to your buddy list.

Keep Jamaa a Friendly Place!

Here are some tips on how to make and keep friends:

- **BE KIND**
  If you get angry, don't hurt someone's feelings.

- **BE RESPECTFUL**
  Everyone is different, and that's okay!

- **DON'T GOSSIP**
  Even when the people you're talking about are not around.

- **BE SUPPORTIVE**
  True friends are happy for you when you get a cool new item or win a game. Congratulate other players, too.

- **A REAL FRIEND WON'T ASK YOU TO BREAK RULES**
  Or lie, cheat, or do any other activities that can hurt you or others.

Real-Life Animal Buddies

IF A TIGER AND A BUNNY CAN BE FRIENDS IN JAMAA, WHAT'S STOPPING a giraffe and a goat from being friends in real life? Nothing! Check out these unusual animal buddies.

Orangutan keeps pet cat!

When Tonda the orangutan's mate died, she became very depressed. She even lost interest in her favorite hobby: painting. But when an orange tabby cat named T.K. came into her life, Tonda found something to smile about again. The orangutan, who lives in a zoo, plays with, pets, and feeds T.K. The cat inspired Tonda to start painting again. Wonder if she's done any portraits of her favorite feline friend?

Duck dotes on dog!

Don't quack up, but Cleo the Labrador retriever mix has a devoted duck pal that follows her everywhere. Sterling the duck sleeps with his head on Cleo's tummy and munches on her dog chow. The pair spend their days exploring their backyard and playing in a pond. Now isn't that just ducky!

Giraffe hangs out with goat!

Gerald the giraffe is the only one of his kind in a wildlife sanctuary in England. The zookeepers moved a friendly goat named Eddie in with him. They've been best buds ever since! Gerald licks Eddie on the head, and the goat hugs the giraffe's long neck with his legs. Don't mess with Gerald's BFF! When Eddie is bothered by the zebras who live at the sanctuary, Gerald chases them away!

Liza

47

perfect Pets

JAMMERS ARE THE BEST PET OWNERS!

Pets can be found throughout the world or in the Claws 'N Paws pet adoption center in Appondale or the Flippers 'N Fins ocean pet center in Crystal Reef.

Once you've adopted your pet, make sure to deck it out in the latest fashions by visiting the Pet Stop! Make your new pet feel at home with den items made especially for your pets at the Pet Den Item Shop.

Some pets can be found only during certain times of the year, while others are for sale only in the Diamond Shop. Occasionally pets will be offered through Animal Jam gift cards. Keep exploring Jamaa until you find your perfect pet!

Monkey

Butterfly

Frog

Kitty

Puppy

Duck

Hamster

Anglerfish

Seahorse

ALPHA TIP

GRAHAM

If you adopt too many pets, you can free your pet by pulling up "Pets" in your inventory and clicking on the button that looks like an open birdcage. Your pet will be returned to the adoption center for another Jammer to adopt.

Snake	Turtle	Bat
Reindeer	Bunny	Hummingbird
Tarantula	Fox	Owl
Tiger	Arctic Wolf	Raccoon
	Jellyfish	

Taking Care of Pets

The pets in Jamaa are pretty low maintenance. If you don't check in with them for a couple of days, they are just fine. But in real life it's very different. Pets are a big responsibility. They need you to take care of them every day for the rest of their lives!

If you are thinking of getting a pet, first you need to think about the right pet for your family. Does anyone have allergies? Do you have a lot of time each day to care for a pet?

Second, you need to make sure you have your parents' permission before bringing a pet into the home. It's a big responsibility and everyone in the family should agree on whether or not they have the time, energy, money, and love for a pet. Between food, supplies, and veterinary care, pets can be expensive.

If you do get a pet, make sure to love it and take good care of it. If you do, you'll have a healthy, happy best friend who will love you back!

Pets Galore: We love our furry friends: 47 percent of U.S. households have a dog!

GAMER'S PARADISE

THE AWESOME GAMES IN JAMAA CAN BE PLAYED SOLO, WITH BUDDIES, OR EVEN WITH YOUR PETS!

GAMES ARE A GREAT WAY TO EARN Gems or just to have some fun! As you journey throughout Jamaa, keep your eyes open for this game controller icon to start playing. Or you can find all of the games in one place, the Sol Arcade in Jamaa Township. This arcade is chock-full of cool games to play, and you can also buy games for your den here, too.

The only games that cannot be found in Sol Arcade are ones you play with your buddies and pets. To play a one-on-one game against one of your buddies, click on his or her name tag to get started. You'll be able to choose from six games: Scooped, Marbles, Shell Game, Rock Paper Scissors, Tic Tac Toe, and Four Gem.

Search Jamaa to play games with some of your pets. You can choose from Disc Toss with your puppy, Ducky Dash with your pet duck, or Sssssnake with your pet snake.

For a list of all the games in Jamaa, turn to page 226.

Animals Play Wild, Too!

CREATURES OF ALL SHAPES AND SIZES LOVE TO PLAY! PLAY KEEPS their minds active and gets them moving—just like us! Check out these cool ways some animals play.

Let the games begin!

These piggies know how to bring home the bacon—and the gold medals—when they compete in the Pig Olympics in Moscow, Russia. The annual event is an Olympic-type competition, which features pig racing, pig swimming, and pigball (think soccer). Russia's specially trained pig athletes live in a complex where vets and coaches attend to their every need.

Dolphin plays with iPad!

Merlin the dolphin has an iPad app especially made for him by his trainer and dolphin researcher, Jack Kassewitz. The app shows an image of an object, like a toy duck, and after Merlin touches the screen with his nose he swims away to find it. It's an iPad scavenger hunt for aquatic animals!

He shoots! He scores!

What do fish do when they have recess from school? Play soccer! Don't believe it? Meet Albert Einstein, a calico fantail goldfish who was trained by his owner to push a ball into a goal. His owner used food pellets to train the fish. Soon Albert was pushing a weighted-down mini soccer ball into a mini goal!

ALPHA TIP

PECK

Earn twice as many Gems as usual when you play the current double Gems game. Look for the banner that says "Gems x2" to rake in those extra Gems!

TRADING

TRADE YOUR UNWANTED ITEMS FOR NEW ONES BY USING JAMAA'S TRADING SYSTEM!

DO YOU HAVE TOO MANY ITEMS IN your collection? Is there stuff you never wear and never want to wear again? Go ahead and trade it! It's a great, safe way to discover new items. Click on your Animal picture in the lower left-hand corner of the screen and click on the tab that says "Trade." You can add items to your trade list so other Jammers can see what you'd like to trade.

You can even check out what other Jammers are offering to trade if you're looking for cool new stuff.

If you're a little confused by the trading system, click on the info button at the bottom of your trade list. You can watch a helpful video that teaches everything about trading. You'll be an expert trader before you know it!

ALPHA TIP

GREELY

Some players might try to unfairly get items from others. That's why Animal Jam HQ created the trading system. If a Jammer wants to trade with you, but asks you to send them a gift through a Jam-A-Gram instead of using the trading system, don't do it. The trading system was invented to keep things fair.

I'll Scratch Your Back If You Scratch Mine!

IN JAMAA, ANIMALS CAN TRADE A PAIR OF WINGS FOR A SOFA, BUT WHAT about in the real world? Animals don't trade objects, but sometimes they help each other out by trading services. When animals do this it's called a symbiotic, or a mutually beneficial, relationship.

Clean my teeth and eat the crumbs!

That arrangement might not sound appealing to you, but to an Egyptian plover it's a dream job. These daring birds hop right inside a crocodile's mouth to eat the tiny bits of food stuck in its teeth. Why doesn't the crocodile eat the plover? Because while the plover is getting a free meal, the crocodile is getting a teeth cleaning that will prevent infections and keep the croc healthy. It's a win-win for both animals!

Help! These parasites are bugging me!

Large mammals, like hippos and water buffaloes, can be crawling with lice, ticks, and other insects. That's not fun. But what's a hippo to do? Find an egret who loves snacking on creepy crawlies! In addition to an all-you-can-eat bug buffet, the birds get the protection of the large animals and a free ride. In exchange, the mammals get relief from the biting and itching caused by those annoying bugs.

Let me drink your sweat and I'll protect you!

There's just something about the dew patches that rain forest caterpillars produce on their backs that are irresistible to certain ants. The ants love drinking the sweet dew so much that they will protect the caterpillar like a bodyguard. They are even known to carry the caterpillar to its nest at night for safety. Wonder if they tuck it in and read it a bedtime story, too?

JAMAA TOWNSHIP

ANIMALS IN JAMAA GATHER TOGETHER EVERY DAY IN THE HEART OF THE LAND.

THIS BUSTLING PLACE IS WHERE JAMMERS GO TO GET the latest news, meet buddies, trade, shop, invite others to parties, see the statue of Mira, and just hang out. In the middle of Jamaa Township is Jammer Central, the place for Jammers to learn about all the cool new things going on in Jamaa.

Look for the bulletin board in Jamaa Township. That's Jammer Central! Here you'll find the Activities Calendar, Featured Video, and Jammer artwork.

Megacity: About 10 percent of Japan's entire population lives in Tokyo.

call this Asian city home! The world's population keeps growing and today's cities are getting bigger and bigger. Cities like Tokyo are called "megacities," which have a population of 10 million or more people. Most of these megacities are located in Asia and the developing world. The U.S. has only two megacities: New York City and Los Angeles. China has the most megacities of any country in the world: four. Some people estimate that by 2030, six out of every ten people all over the world will live in a city. Jamaa Township is like some of these major cities, with shops, places to get together, and lots of exciting action!

You can read howls from other residents of Jamaa as well as submit one of your own. Lots of animals visit Jamaa Township every day, but it doesn't compare to the city that has the most people living in it: Tokyo, Japan. More than 13 million people

IN THE FIELD WITH DR. BRADY BARR

WILDLIFE IN THE CITY

Jamaa Township may be running wild with all different kinds of animals, but what about the town or city you call home? For people who live in rural areas, it's not so strange to have bears or coyotes as neighbors. But people living in cities are discovering wild animals in their neighborhoods, too.

The cause? Sometimes it's the lure of an easy meal. Gardens, trashcans, and bird feeders offer a smorgasbord for animals to feast on. Other times it's because the animals simply have no place else to go as humans build on the land the animals live on.

The best way to avoid having a critter as a neighbor is not to attract them in the first place. So keep garbage secured, pet food inside, and take down bird feeders in the spring.

Djemaa el Fna Square's market is open late into the night.

Market stand filled with dried fruit

STEP BACK IN TIME AND ENTER an ancient world of mysterious bazaars at the Djemaa el Fna Square, an open-air market in Marrakech, Morocco. This North African souk, or market, attracts visitors from around the world. And it's no wonder! During the day, it's an exciting shopper's paradise. If you can find your way through the labyrinth of ancient city walls, you'll discover alleys filled with shops that specialize in different items. Choose from hundreds of vendors selling jewelry, spices, carpets, and furniture, along with tourist trinkets. Listen to a story-teller spin tales of Moroccan legends

Djemaa el Fna Square
Bustling Bazaar

while you snack on freshly squeezed juice and succulent Moroccan dates.

When night falls, the market transforms into a colorful circus. Snake charmers, fortune-tellers, perform-ing monkeys, musicians, dancers, and acrobats entertain the crowds much as they did in 1000 B.C. when Marrakech was a route for caravan traders.

If you're looking for a real-life place that is as colorful and magi-cal as Jamaa Town-ship, Djemaa el Fna Square might be it!

Moroccan Delicacy: A chef sells cooked snails at the bazaar.

so you want to be a BUNNY?

LeT's see you HOP!

OR BETTER YET, LET'S see you run. Rabbits are famous for hopping, but did you know when they really get hopping they can reach a speed of 18 miles an hour (29 kph)? That's fast!

Rabbits are sometimes referred to as hares, but they are not the same animals. Hares are related to rabbits but generally have longer ears and hind feet than rabbits.

There are 28 species of rabbit, but the eastern cottontail is one of the most common. Cottontails range in color from reddish brown to gray, but all have the same adorable white "cotton ball" tail for which they are named.

Hefty Hearing: All rabbits have long ears. If you were a tasty treat to most predators, you'd want to hear if someone was sneaking up on you, too!

Are You a Bunny?

THIS IS A GREAT ANIMAL FOR JAMMERS WHO ARE ENERGETIC! LOVE TO DANCE? WATCH YOUR BUNNY'S EARS FLY WHEN DANCING IN ANIMAL JAM.

STATS

COTTONTAIL RABBIT

▸ **TYPE:** Mammal
▸ **DIET:** Grasses, herbs, buds, twigs, bark, and garden treats such as peas and lettuce
▸ **LIFE SPAN:** Less than 3 years
▸ **SIZE:** 15.5 to 18.75 inches (39.5 to 47.7 cm)
▸ **WEIGHT:** 28 to 54 ounces (800 to 1,533 g)
▸ **WHERE THEY LIVE:** Canada, South America, United States

ANIMAL DANCE PARTY!

Let's Move and Shake!

DANCING IS REALLY FUN AS YOUR ANIMAL JAM animal in Jamaa. Think you can dance? Check out these real-world animal dancers!

Jitterbugs!

When bees dance, the tune they're listening to isn't music; it's the rumbling of their stomachs! A bee's carefully choreographed dance is a way to let other bees know where food can be found. When the bee shimmies in a straight line, he's pointing in the direction of the meal by using the position of the sun to navigate.

Dancing in the Name of Love

One of the most amazing dances in the animal kingdom is performed by birds-of-paradise. There are more than three dozen species of this bird, but they all have one thing in common: a feather-fluffing, body-shaking dance that resembles no other! The males of the species do this ornate dance in hopes of enticing a picky female to mate.

DESTINATION A.J.

CLUB GEOZ

Find the most jammin' dance parties in Jamaa at Club Geoz! Head for the building with the musical note on the door in Jamaa Township to start grooving. While you'll love the funky music playing and will want to dance the day away, make some time to stop by the Photo Booth. Choose a background, strike a pose, pick a cool saying, and you'll have a cool photo you can download and share!

All the animals in Jamaa are unique even when it comes to dancing! Each animal has its own special dance style.

Groovy Sea Lion

After being stranded in California, U.S.A., Ronan the sea lion was rescued by researchers. They taught her to bob her head along to simple beats. Ronan now moves in time to more complex rhythms, like songs by the Backstreet Boys!

SIR GILBERT

ALPHA TIP

The party really gets going when lots of Jammers hit the dance floor in Club Geoz. Throw a dance party there to see what happens!

59

Green Cities

COOL PLACES THAT CUT DOWN ON POLLUTION

ECO-CITIES ARE BEING CREATED around the globe as more and more people look for ways to live without harming the environment or using up natural resources.

One example of a city trying to reduce pollution and waste is Vancouver, Canada. Its admirable goal is to be the greenest city in the world by 2020! So far Vancouver has planted more than 12,500 trees, decreased total water consumption by 16 percent, added 158 miles (255 km) of bike routes to the city, increased park space, and added public charging stations for electric vehicles.

Other places face some challenging problems. Air pollution is a big problem in all of China. To make the air and water cleaner and healthier in the entire country, the government is trying to curtail the burning of coal, limit the amount of vehicle traffic, and close some factories that contribute to the smog.

But eco-cities are being built in China, too! In Sino-Singapore Tianjin the government is building a brand-new city in the hope that one day it will be home to 350,000 residents who live in energy-efficient buildings; walk, bike, or use electric vehicles powered by renewable energy; and recycle waste and water.

Eco-Charge: Electric-vehicle charging stations are appearing in many places around the world for zero-emissions cars.

Are You a Panda?

IF YOU FIND YOURSELF HESITATING BEFORE DIVING INTO THE ACTION, YOU'VE GOT A LOT IN COMMON WITH THE SHY PANDA! THIS IS A GREAT ANIMAL FOR JAMMERS WHO ARE QUIET AND LOVE EXPLORING ON THEIR OWN.

STATS

GIANT PANDA

- **TYPE:** Mammal
- **DIET:** Mostly bamboo, occasionally other vegetation, fish, or small animals
- **LIFE SPAN:** 20 years
- **SIZE:** 4 to 5 feet (1.2 to 1.5 m)
- **WEIGHT:** 165 to 300 pounds (75 to 136 kg)
- **STATUS:** Endangered
- **WHERE THEY LIVE:** Central China

SO YOU WANT TO BE A PANDA?

THEN GET MUNCHING!

A TYPICAL GIANT PANDA spends 12 hours a day eating bamboo. Pandas have to chow down on about 28 pounds (13 kg) of the woody grasses daily because they digest only about a fifth of what they eat. Pandas' broad, flat molars are perfect for crushing the bamboo shoots, leaves, and stems that make up the majority of their diet. But all that eating leads to another call of nature. Pandas poop dozens of times a day!

Pandas live in the dense bamboo forests of central China. But pandas in the wild are in trouble. There are only about 1,000 giant pandas left in the wild. To help protect the panda, the Chinese government and conservation organizations have created sheltered areas and breeding centers for them.

BUILDING the First Cities

THERE HAVE BEEN MANY KINDS OVER HUNDREDS OF YEARS.

WE DON'T THINK OF CITIES AND FARMS as having much in common, but when early humans learned how to improve the ways they farmed and cared for animals, cities were born! In the early Neolithic period, about 9000 to 3000 B.C., people did live in villages. But they'd have to move periodically to search for better soil in which to plant their crops. This is known as a nomadic lifestyle. Imagine having to pack up your entire town and take off!

When people began to figure out better ways to cultivate the land and domesticate animals, they were able to stay put in permanent communities. Humans figured this out between 5000 and 3500 B.C. Better farming meant more food, so not everyone had to labor as farmers. Some were able to work instead as potters and weavers. Residents of the earliest urban cities were able to form governments, learn to read and write, and invent new things, which was really tough to do when they lived in seminomadic villages.

DESTINATION A.J.

SHOPPING SPOTS IN JAMAA

Jamaa Township is full of cool stores with items galore! Visit these shops to find awesome accessories for your animal and decorations for your den!

Jam Mart Furniture

Jam Mart Clothing

Sol Arcade

Cool Buys: The Diamond Shop has the most elite items for sale.

Shop 'Til You Drop!

You can buy some amazing items in Jamaa, like crystal statues, golden thrones, and a royal tiara. But there are some pretty incredible things you can buy in the real world, too.

"Potty" like a billionaire with a solid-gold toilet worth $37 million.

Talk about pampered living! In 2012, U.S. pet owners spent $53 billion on their pets!

$150,000 is a lot for a cupcake that you've got to pick all the diamonds off of before you can eat it—what a pain!

This $70,000 bear has diamond and sapphire eyes, gold leaf in its fur, and a gold nose!

For $1.75 million, you can own the sQuba car and go for an underwater drive.

A blinged-out and bedazzled Mercedes-Benz will cost you $1 million.

Sir Gilbert

ALPHA TIP

Every Monday, one super-rare item is for sale in one of the shops around Jamaa.

WHO WORE it BEST?

IN JAMAA, WHO CAN PULL OFF THE CRAZIEST OUTFIT?

Everyone! With tons of fun clothing and accessories to choose from, you'll always be best dressed. Check out how these cheetahs and foxes make fashion fierce. Which do you like the best?

Feel like being the class clown? Crack your friends up in this goofy getup!

With this crazy combination of clothing, you'll be ready for anything!

CHEETAH

Get ready to sail the high seas of fashion in this daring ensemble.

You're sure to steal the spotlight with these flashy accessories.

Feeling tough? This outfit will give you plenty of attitude!

FUN FACT

SOME PET OWNERS USE HARMLESS FOOD COLORING TO DYE THEIR PETS CRAZY COLORS. DOGS HAVE BEEN DYED TO LOOK LIKE TIGERS, PANDAS, AND MORE!

THESE SPARKLES PUT ME OVER THE TOP!

Who knows what you'll get up to in this dashing jacket and roguish hat!

Set off for your next wild adventure in this stylish explorer's outfit.

FOX

You'll be the ultimate trend-setter with this color-coordinated skirt set.

Think foxes are cute? Think again when you're wearing this fierce dragon costume.

Show off your mysterious nature in an elegant cape and matching earmuffs.

Crazy Camouflage

When you think of bold patterns, do you think of a cheetah's spots or a tiger's stripes? While these patterns might stand out on humans, they actually serve a much different purpose in the wild. These animals' coats act as a camouflage, allowing them to hunt prey or hide from predators.

Even though they seem flashy, a cheetah's tan and black spots blend in easily with the dry grasses of the savanna, allowing cheetahs to move unnoticed through an open plain. A tiger's stripes work similarly; the vertical pattern of the stripes lets the big cat blend in with the tall grasses of the jungle.

River Race

JAMAA DERBY

 DUCKY DASH

GReaT GaMeS
IN JAMAA TOWNSHIP

65

LOST TEMPLE OF ZIOS

A mysterious ruin in a jungle land awaits you in Jamaa—the Lost Temple of Zios. If you're ready to uncover this land's secrets, **Let's explore the forest!**

WHEN YOU FIRST ENTER THE DARK AND MYSTERIOUS rain forest, the sounds of insects humming, birds calling, and tree branches rustling meet your ears. But as you move in closer, a hush falls across the land. You get that funny feeling that someone, somewhere is watching you, but you're not quite sure who—or what—it is.

The truth is that potentially millions of eyes are studying your every move once you set foot in a rain forest.

Even though rain forests take up only about 6 percent of the land on Earth, they are home to about half the world's plant and animal species! Millions of insects, reptiles, amphibians, birds, and mammals live in the rain forest. If you're not a fan of creepy-crawly creatures, this is not the place for you! The most common type of animal found here are invertebrates, which include insects, arachnids (yep, that means spiders and scorpions!), and worms.

Animals are not the only ones to call the rain forest home. Tribal people live in these tropical forests and survive off the land, getting food, shelter, and medicine from their surroundings.

In the rain forest of Jamaa, you'll find all kinds of creatures, including some sights you'd never see in a real rain forest—like a seal taking its pet puppy for a stroll!

DESTINATION A.J.

BRADY'S LAB

Deep in the Lost Temple of Zios, you'll find National Geographic Explorer Dr. Brady Barr's laboratory. Brady is a herpetologist—a scientist who studies amphibians and reptiles. His lab is where he hangs out and performs his experiments. But Brady's job isn't all about sitting at a desk. Check out his videos to see close encounters with real, sharp-toothed wildlife. You can visit anytime to see all the tools he uses to learn about our planet's amazing creatures. In fact, he'll even let you explore the gear, gadgets, and gizmos he has in his lab—like his croc suit! Tag along with Brady on one of his expeditions. Help him track down giant snakes like pythons and boa constrictors!

Wandering spider

Lush Rain Forest:
Lots of plant life grows in this temperate rain forest in Victoria, Australia.

DESTINATION A.J.

BRADY'S THEATER

Make sure to stop by the movie theater. Watch videos of Brady answering Jammers' questions about animals, including everything from "Why do dogs pant?" to "Do worms have eyes?" Have a burning question? Submit one of your own!

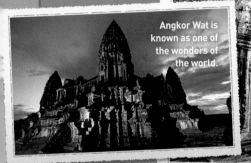

Angkor Wat is known as one of the wonders of the world.

Strangler figs grow wild over the ancient Preah Khan Temple in Angkor.

WHAT'S ONE WAY TO MAKE SURE NO one ever forgets you? Try building the world's largest religious monument! That's what Suryavarman II did. He was king of the Khmer Empire during the first half of the 12th century when he ordered construction to begin on Angkor Wat, which means "temple city." Jamaa's Lost Temple of Zios is based on this real-life ancient place. It was built in the tropical rain forest of Cambodia in Southeast Asia over 800 years ago.

Suryavarman II wanted to re-create heaven on Earth when building Angkor Wat. So he designed it to look like Mount Meru, the legendary home of the gods in Hindu mythology. A central monument symbolizes the mythical mountain, while five towers represent its five peaks.

When you travel around the Lost Temple of Zios, you'll notice ancient statues and stone murals peeking out from the forest's foliage. These were inspired by the carvings and sculptures in Angkor Wat. It took about 5,000 artisans and 50,000 laborers over 30 years to build and sculpt the temple complex and the many statues found there!

When it was the heart of the Khmer Empire, up to one million people lived in Angkor. Today, about two million visitors come every year to see this architectural wonder. Yet some still call this ancient city home. Villages can be found throughout Angkor where people live today. Many of them are descended from the people who built, lived in, and worked in Angkor so many years ago.

Hindu Temple: Statues and sculptures depicting scenes from Hindu religion are all over the city of Angkor.

SO YOU WANT TO BE A TIGER?

SHOW OFF YOUR STRIPES!

SIBERIAN TIGER

- **TYPE:** Mammal
- **DIET:** Deer, elk, and wild boar
- **LIFE SPAN:** 8 to 10 years in the wild
- **SIZE:** 10.75 feet (3.3 m)
- **WEIGHT:** Up to 660 pounds (300 kg)
- **STATUS:** Endangered
- **WHERE THEY LIVE:** Asia

TIGERS ARE THE WORLD'S LARGEST cats and are easily recognized by their beautiful reddish-orange coat with dark stripes. Their lovely coats aren't just for show; they serve as camouflage when the tiger is hunting. A tiger's stripes are like fingerprints. No two tigers have exactly the same stripes!

But tigers also have it tough. This big cat has a successful hunt only about once out of every 20 attempts. When it does make a kill, tigers have been known to eat up to 60 pounds (27 kg) of meat in one night!

There are six species of tiger and they are all endangered. The cause: the hunting of tigers and the destruction of their habitat. Many conservation programs have been put in place to save these animals.

Are You a Tiger?

IF YOU WANT TO BE A TIGER, THROW BACK YOUR HEAD AND ROAR! KNOWN FOR THEIR HUNTING SKILLS AND STRENGTH, TIGERS MAKE A GREAT ANIMAL FOR JAMMERS WHO ARE PATIENT AND POWERFUL.

IN THE FIELD WITH DR. BRADY BARR

SPLASHING AROUND

Cats are notorious for disliking water. Have you ever tried to give one a bath? But tigers are different—they love water!

Not only are tigers good swimmers, but the big cats seem to really enjoy splashing around.

They'll swim in order to hunt or to get from place to place, but tigers have been observed playing in the water, too. They've also been seen taking satisfying soaks in watering holes to cool off and relax. It's

almost as if tigers have their very own hot tubs. Maybe they'd enjoy a day at the spa, too!

71

Flower power!

Special plants save the world!

THE AMAZON RAIN FOREST ALONE IS home to over 40,000 plant species. Now that's a lot of flower power! More and more, scientists are discovering that rain forest plants are very powerful. In fact, about 70 percent of plants with cancer-fighting properties come from the rain forest. And that's not all. Rain forest plants have been used to treat malaria, heart disease, diabetes, high blood pressure, and arthritis as well as many other ailments. Rain forest plants and herbs are also used in foods and cosmetics.

What makes plants found in the rain forest so special? Rain forests are crawling with insects that like to munch on the bountiful salad bar of vegetation around them. To protect themselves from all those tiny chomping jaws, plants develop chemicals to make themselves stronger and to ward off insect predators. It's these chemicals that researchers are using in medicines. New plants are always being discovered, making the rain forest a place that could potentially hold the cure for many diseases.

ALPHA TIP

COSMO

Legend has it that if three Jammers sleep next to the broken statue in the center of the Lost Temple of Zios, Phantoms will appear. Be on your guard!

The Temple of Kukulkan is the largest temple in Chichén Itzá.

Chacmool Statue:
Statues depicting people sitting on the ground are thought to have been used for sacrifices or offerings to the gods.

THOUSANDS OF JAMMERS VISIT the Lost Temple of Zios every day, but there's another temple that attracts many visitors from around the world: the Temple of Kukulkan. It's located in the ruins of the ancient Maya city, Chichén Itzá, in Mexico.

The Maya Empire included territory in southern Mexico, Guatemala, and northern Belize. At the height of their power in sixth century A.D., the Maya excelled at mathematics, architecture, agriculture, pottery, astronomy, and calendar-making. They are also noted for having the only known written language in Mesoamerica.

The Temple of Kukulkan, also known as El Castillo, is a stair-stepped pyramid with a shrine on the top that's a testament to the importance of Maya astronomy. Its four sides face north, south, east, and west. The stairways on each face of the pyramid have 91 steps. When all four of the stairways are combined with the step on the top platform, it adds up to 365, the number of days in a year. That's not the only interesting detail. When shadows cast by the setting sun fall upon the temple during the spring and autumnal equinoxes, they resemble a snake crawling down the staircases! It's believed the temple was built to create this effect because of Quetzalcóatl, a feathered serpent who was a major deity in Maya religion. A carving of Quetzalcóatl also adorns the top of the pyramid.

Serpent God:
Quetzalcóatl was a snake, and many of the statues at Kukulkan are serpentine.

Temple of Kukulkan

Shrine to the Gods

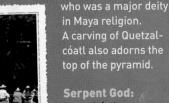

TROPICAL or TEMPERATE?

RAIN FORESTS ARE FOUND ALL OVER THE WORLD!

THE TERM "RAIN FOREST" CONJURES UP images of hot and steamy jungles teeming with exotic animals and plants. If that's true, then how can there be rain forests in Alaska? Rain forests generally have at least 100 inches (254 cm) of rainfall per year.

Tropical rain forests, like the Amazon rain forest in South America, are close to the Equator. Temperate rain forests, such as Olympic National Park in Washington, U.S.A., are located farther away from the Equator. Temperatures in tropical rain

forests are warm, whereas temperate forests are cool. While hundreds of different tree species flourish in tropical rain forests, only about 10 to 20 varieties grow in a temperate rain forest. Trees in a temperate forest can be up to 1,000 years old! That's very old compared to the youngsters in the tropical rain forests, who on average are 50 to 100 years old.

Tropical and temperate rain forests may have some differences but they have one thing in common: they're both beautiful!

Keel-billed toucan

THE LARGEST AND oldest tropical rain forest in the world is the amazing Amazon rain forest. This South American forest covers an area of 2.3 million square miles (6 million sq km) and spills into Brazil, Bolivia, Peru, Ecuador, Colombia, Venezuela, Guyana, Suriname, and French Guiana. It's huge—and ancient! The Amazon rain forest is believed to be 100 million years old. It's also home to

Jaguar

Amazon Rain Forest
Amazing Tropical Home

a diverse range of species of insects, plants, birds, and other forms of life, many of which are not found anywhere else in the world.

While the Amazon rain forest is busy being home to all these animal, plant, bird,

CHAMBER OF KNOWLEDGE

A building sits deep in the rain forest, overgrown with green vines. As you approach the stone door, a python slithers next to it, its tongue flicking in and out. As you feel your heart beat faster in your chest, the door opens as if by magic. You quickly run inside and find yourself in the mysterious Chamber of Knowledge!

On the first floor of this ancient building is a library filled with National Geographic books. Learn more about the wild world around you or continue up to the second floor to explore the artifacts and statues stored here. Make sure you walk all the way to the left of the room to find the final staircase leading to the third floor and the Mystery Emporium.

Amazing items beyond your wildest dreams are for sale in this shop. Magical objects from faraway places and statues of the Alphas are all part of the Emporium's inventory.

and insect species, it's also performing an important job as an air purifier. The plants in the Amazon absorb carbon dioxide in the air. Carbon dioxide is a greenhouse gas responsible for climate change. All together, the world's rain forests absorb billions of tons of carbon dioxide found in our atmosphere.

But this vitally important part of the world is in danger. During the past 40 years, close to 20 percent of the Amazon rain forest has been cut down. About 80,000 acres (32,400 ha) of tropical rain forest are destroyed daily, and experts believe the world is losing 135 plant, animal, and insect species every day as the forests fall.

Many organizations are working to protect the rain forests and the animals like the jaguar, howler monkey, tapir, red deer, capybara, manatee, and toucan that live here. You can lend a hand by doing something as simple as reusing and recycling paper. Every bit helps!

Strawberry poison dart frog

Howler monkey

WHO WOULD HAVE THOUGHT A TROPICAL RAIN forest has something in common with a cake? It does—layers! But unless you like munching on insects and leaves, the layers in a rain forest aren't quite as tasty. They're invaluable to the animals that live there, however.

Rain Forest Layers

EMERGENT LAYER
There is plenty of sunshine to be found here on the treetops. Emergent trees can tower up to 200 feet (61 m) tall, almost as high as a 20-story building! Butterflies, eagles, bats, and some monkeys make their home in the emergent layer.

CANOPY LAYER
The primary layer, the canopy forms the roof of the rain forest and is a maze of leaves and branches. But the three-toed sloths, snakes, monkeys, toucans, lizards, and frogs that live here have no problem finding their way around.

UNDERSTORY LAYER
This is where things begin to get dark, because little sunshine can get through the canopy. Plants grow large here. Many insects can be found in this hot and humid layer, along with jaguars, tree frogs, leopards, owls, and bats.

FOREST FLOOR
It's damp and dark with little vegetation growing except for some moss and the giant roots of the rain forest trees. Things decay very quickly in this layer, and the floor is filled with twigs and decomposing leaves. Giant anteaters call the forest floor home and share it with other large animals like jaguars and anaconda snakes.

SO YOU WANT TO BE A MONKEY?

GO BANANAS IN JAMAA!

THE WORLD IS FILLED WITH monkeys! There are nearly 200 species of these cute mammals.

Monkeys are divided into two groups: Old World and New World. Old World monkeys, like baboons and colobuses, live mostly in parts of Africa and Asia, while New World monkeys live in Central and South America.

If you step into the forest and hear screeches and barks, it's most likely coming from the noisy spider monkey! These monkeys live in tropical rain forests and are perfectly built for a life in the canopy layer of the forest. Their long, lanky limbs and gripping tails let them move easily from branch to branch.

Monkey Features: New World monkeys, like this spider monkey, have large prehensile tails that they use for traveling through trees.

STATS

SPIDER MONKEY

- **TYPE:** Mammal
- **DIET:** Nuts, fruits, leaves, bird eggs, and spiders
- **LIFE SPAN:** 22 years
- **SIZE:** 14 to 26 inches (35 to 66 cm)
- **WEIGHT:** 13.25 pounds (6 kg)
- **STATUS:** Endangered
- **WHERE THEY LIVE:** Central and South America

Are You a Monkey?

KNOWN FOR THEIR PLAYFULNESS AND INTELLIGENCE, MONKEYS ARE A GREAT ANIMAL FOR JAMMERS WHO ARE FUNNY AND SMART!

Bonus! For more fun identify all the reptiles in this scene. How many are there?

Rain Forest Search

SEEK AND FIND

Can you find the objects in this jungle scene? Look carefully!

1	sloth	1	gorilla
3	butterflies	3	birds
1	tarantula	1	pair of binoculars
4	snakes	1	giant fly
9	frogs		

Find the answers on page 231.

Great Games
IN THE LOST TEMPLE OF ZIOS

Temple of Trivia

MARA SAYS

GEM BALL

FALLING PHANTOMS

Brady Barr's CHEMISTRY SET

APPONDALE

GO ON SAFARI WITH SOME OF THE MOST AMAZING CREATURES IN JAMAA!

HEN YOU STEP INTO APPONDALE, THE VISTA STRETCHES for as far as the eye can see. If you perch on the rocks next to the Claws 'N Paws tree house and keep looking into the distance, some of the animals that call the savanna home will show themselves!

A wildebeest might come to graze on the grass, or a zebra could go racing past. If you get too hot animal-watching under the bright sun, wallow in Appondale's mud pool to cool off. African animals like the warthog, elephant, and rhino do this all the time in real life to beat the heat!

Great Migration: Many African animals migrate thousands of miles every year, like these in Serengeti National Park.

CLAWS 'N PAWS

The pets in Jamaa are so adorable; you'll want to adopt them all! The Claws 'N Paws adoption center is located inside the cool tree house in Appondale. The tree is a baobab tree—a common sight on the savanna. These smart trees store moisture and nutrients deep in their roots that they can use during times of drought!

Pets can be found all throughout Jamaa, but in Claws 'N Paws you can find a bunch of them under one baobab roof! Snakes, kitties, puppies, turtles, frogs, ducks, butterflies, and hamsters are all available for adoption here.

But be warned. The mud can have an interesting effect on your animal!

Appondale is a lot like the savanna grasslands found in Africa. When an area is covered with grasses rather than large shrubs or trees, it's considered grassland. Savannas are mostly grassy areas but do

Tall Drinker: Giraffes don't have to bend their knees to drink at the water hole. Good thing they have long necks!

have scattered trees, much like the panorama in Appondale. Savannas provide an area of transition between desert and forest.

The African savannas are huge and cover about five million miles of central Africa—that's about half of the continent's surface! Large savannas are also found in Australia, South America, and India.

The recipe for making a savanna includes warm temperatures, a rainy season, and then a long period of drought.

ALPHA TIP

COSMO

Pet games are a fun way to earn Gems, but did you know that you can also play them to earn neat effects for your pet? Just collect 100 golden items with any pet to unlock a cool effect!

Lions take a break in Serengeti National Park, Tanzania.

Flamingos flock at Lake Nakuru, Kenya, Africa.

The Serengeti

The African Safari

COME ALONG ON A FASCINATING safari through one of the oldest ecosystems on Earth. Get an up-close look at wildebeests, gazelles, lions, zebras, and hyenas as you take a tour of the Serengeti! Jamaa's Appondale is based on this real-life grassland.

Located in Tanzania, Africa, the climate, vegetation, and fauna of this 12,000-square mile (31,080-sq km) ecosystem has barely changed in the past million years. The local people, the Maasai, gave this seemingly boundless land its name, which means "endless plains."

During the Great Migration, over a million wildebeests, hundreds of thousands of zebras, and numerous gazelles and other animals migrate from the southeast of Serengeti toward Kenya and back to the Serengeti in search of rich grasslands and water. Visitors come from around the world to witness this spectacular sight. The instinct to migrate is so strong that nothing will stop the animals, which face predators, drought, and perilous river crossings to reach their destination. To help preserve the incredible array of wildlife found here, the Serengeti National Park and wildlife refuge was created in 1951. The park covers an area of 5,700 square miles (14,763 sq km) and is home to elephants, lions, ostriches, baboons, rhinoceroses, hippopotamuses, giraffes, cheetahs, crocodiles, leopards, and flamingos—animals you'd normally only see in a zoo!

Africa's People: The Maasai people live in parts of the Serengeti.

SO YOU WANT TO BE A CHEETAH?

SHOW OFF YOUR SPEED!

IF YOU'RE A SPEED DEMON WITH SMOKIN' SNEAKERS, YOU'VE GOT a lot in common with the cheetah! The cheetah is the world's fastest land mammal and can go from 0 to 60 miles an hour (0 to 97 kph) in only 3 seconds! Most cars can't accelerate that fast. This daytime hunter has a lot in its favor: exceptional eyesight, a spotted coat for camouflage, and of course its scary speed! What's an antelope to do? Not much. The cheetah silently stalks its prey and gets as close as possible before bolting toward it at lightning speeds. It knocks its prey to the ground before clamping on its throat with its teeth.

Today, cheetahs are in a different race and it's not a good one. They are racing toward extinction. These cats are losing their habitat and the numbers of the animals they prey on are declining. Botswana, Africa, is home to one of the last free-ranging cheetah populations in the world.

Are You a Cheetah?

IF YOU'RE THE TYPE OF PERSON THAT EVERYONE WANTS ON THEIR TEAM FOR A RELAY RACE, YOU'VE GOT A LOT IN COMMON WITH THE SPEEDY CHEETAH! THIS IS A GREAT ANIMAL FOR JAMMERS WHO ARE FAST AND FURIOUS!

Hunter Games: Baby cheetahs will live with Mom for up to a year and a half, playing games with her and their siblings that teach them to become hunters.

WAS THAT A BIRD? OR A PLANE?

No, that blur of pure speed is a cheetah, and boy, is it fast! But how does the cheetah stack up against the world's fastest dog? Like the cheetah, the greyhound has a small head, large chest, and a tiny waist built for sprinting at swift speeds. These dogs have been clocked as fast as 43 miles an hour (69 kph). A cheetah would win that race, but a greyhound would have the advantage over a cheetah that lived in a zoo its entire life. Captive cheetahs are recorded at running at speeds of 38 miles an hour (61 kph), nowhere near the 60 miles an hour (97 kph) of those in the wild. Researchers believe the zoo cheetahs aren't as fast as their counterparts in the wild because they've never had to run to catch food.

STATS

CHEETAH

- **TYPE:** Mammal
- **DIET:** Hares, impalas, wildebeest calves, and gazelles
- **LIFE SPAN:** 10 to 12 years
- **SIZE:** 3.5 to 4.5 feet (1.1 to 1.4 m)
- **WEIGHT:** 77 to 143 pounds (35 to 65 kg)
- **STATUS:** Vulnerable
- **WHERE THEY LIVE:** Africa and one small group in Iran

85

ENDANGERED
ANIMALS OF AFRICA

CREATURES THAT NEED OUR HELP!

WHEN AN ANIMAL IS CLASSIFIED AS endangered or threatened, it means it is in danger of going extinct, or disappearing from the planet forever. They include many iconic animals such as the African wild dog, rhinoceros, cheetah, chimpanzee, lion, African elephant, plus several species of hyena, gazelle, and lemur.

The loss of habitat and prey is a reason many of these animals are endangered, but some of them face a bigger threat: poachers. Rhinoceros are killed for their horns, elephants for their ivory tusks, and leopards for their beautiful fur coats.

There is hope. Conservation organizations are working to form antipoaching patrols, toughen laws against the illegal wildlife trade, and encourage wildlife tourism to local communities who live alongside endangered species. Once the numbers of a threatened species rise to healthy levels, they can be taken off the endangered list.

Chimpanzee

Dangerous Creatures

What's the most dangerous animal in Africa? Hint: It's not a lion.

Hippo

Territorial hippos will kill any creatures, including crocodiles, that venture into their territories or get too close to their babies. Walk across the wrong riverbank, and the enormous hippo can run over 20 miles an hour (32 kph) to chase you down!

Mosquito

The most deadly creature is way smaller than a hippo. It's a tiny insect that kills more people than any other creature. The mosquito spreads malaria and other diseases that kill millions of Africans every year.

Black Mamba

This aggressive creature is the largest venomous snake in Africa and can grow up to 14 feet (4.3 m) long! When cornered, these deadly snakes can strike furiously up to 12 times. That's enough venom to kill a dozen people within an hour!

African wild dog

Rhinoceros

Lion

Cheetah

Cuvier's gazelle

Lemur

Leopard

African elephant

CONSERVATION MUSEUM

We know it can be really sad to learn about all the animals that are endangered in the world. We've got some good news—Jamaa has a special place where Jammers can help these animals! The Conservation Museum in Appondale is filled with exhibits and information about endangered animals in the wild. Watch movies about big cats throughout the world and donate Gems to help conservation efforts. And you won't want to miss the Museum Shop located in the museum. It sells awesome hats (like the Panda Hat, the Bunny Hat, and the Eagle Hat) for animals to wear. Before you go, stop by the table in the middle of the room to print out fun animal info sheets!

SO YOU WANT TO BE AN ELEPHANT?

Raise your trunk!

ELEPHANTS ARE THE LARGEST living land animals in the world and are known for their long trunks. In addition to giving hugs, elephants' trunks are used for drinking, smelling, trumpeting, and grabbing. These useful appendages contain about 100,000 different muscles.

There are two main species of elephant: the African elephant and the Asian elephant. In addition, the smaller African forest elephant, a subspecies of the African elephant, lives in rain forests. African elephants are larger than their Asian cousins. Both species have tusks they use to dig for food and water and strip bark from trees. Males will use their tusks to fight each other. The tusks are made out of ivory, which has made elephants a target of poachers.

Big Eaters: Elephants can eat 300 pounds (136 kg) of food in one day.

STATS

AFRICAN ELEPHANT
- **TYPE:** Mammal
- **DIET:** Roots, grasses, fruit, and bark
- **LIFE SPAN:** Up to 70 years
- **SIZE:** Height at the shoulder: 8.2 to 13 feet (2.5 to 4 m)
- **WEIGHT:** 5,000 to 14,000 pounds (2,268 to 6,350 kg)
- **STATUS:** Vulnerable
- **WHERE THEY LIVE:** Africa

Are You an Elephant?
IF YOU LOVE TO SPEND TIME WITH YOUR FAMILY AND FRIENDS, YOU'VE GOT A LOT IN COMMON WITH AN ELEPHANT! THIS ANIMAL IS GREAT FOR JAMMERS WHO ARE FRIENDLY AND LOVING.

IT DOESN'T TAKE MUCH TO make a hot-headed rhinoceros angry. At any sign of a threat, they'll attack.

But we can't blame these big beasts for cases of mistaken identity. They have poor eyesight and are just as likely to rush a rock as they are another animal.

There are five species of these horned mammals, whose name comes from the Greek word *rhino*, which means nose, and *ceros*, which means horn. If a rhinoceros's horn breaks off, it can grow back. It is made mostly of keratin, which can be found in your own fingernails!

Are You a Rhino?

IF YOU TEND TO CHARGE INTO SITUATIONS BEFORE ASKING QUESTIONS, YOU'VE GOT A LOT IN COMMON WITH A RHINO! THIS ANIMAL IS GREAT FOR JAMMERS WHO ARE HOT-TEMPERED AND TOUGH!

...or a RHINO?

Get ready to charge!

Fierce Moms: Female rhinos aggressively protect their young from enemies while teaching them how to survive.

STATS

BLACK RHINOCEROS

- ▸ TYPE: Mammal
- ▸ DIET: Trees, bushes, leaves, and fruit
- ▸ LIFE SPAN: Up to 35 years
- ▸ SIZE: 4.5 to 6 feet (1.4 to 1.8 m)
- ▸ WEIGHT: 1,760 to 3,080 pounds (800 to 1,400 kg)
- ▸ STATUS: Endangered
- ▸ WHERE THEY LIVE: Africa

89

Fire: THE SAVANNA'S FRIEND?

WILDFIRES WORK TO KEEP THE SAVANNA HEALTHY!

IT SOUNDS ODD, BUT WILDFIRES ACTUALLY PLAY AN important part in the savanna's biodiversity. At the height of the dry season, fires often occur that keep the savanna healthy. The fire kills seedlings, stops grasses and trees from growing too tall, and prevents forests from spreading into the savanna. It also stops the savanna from intruding into the forest, so wildfires help maintain the borders between these two lands.

Most animals escape the fire. Smaller animals hide underground, while larger ones are able to run away. Insects, lizards, and mice are the biggest casualties of the blazes, as birds flock to feast on these critters when they try to escape the flames.

SO YOU WANT TO BE A GiRAFFE?

EVERYONE WiLL LOOK UP to YOU!

Lengthy Tongue: If a leaf is a little too high, a giraffe puts its 21-inch (53-cm)-long tongue to use!

STATS

GIRAFFE

- ▸ TYPE: Mammal
- ▸ DIET: Leaves and buds, particularly from acacia trees
- ▸ LIFE SPAN: 25 years
- ▸ SIZE: 14 to 19 feet (4 to 6 m)
- ▸ WEIGHT: 1,750 to 2,800 pounds (794 to 1,270 kg)
- ▸ WHERE THEY LIVE: Africa

THERE ARE PERKS TO being the tallest mammal in the world! They can reach leaves and buds in treetops that most other animals can't. Giraffes munch on hundreds of pounds of leaves a week and get most of the water they need from their plant diet. Standing up to 19 feet (6 m) high also allows giraffes to have an excellent field of vision, giving them an advantage when it comes to spotting a predator approaching from a distance. Lions don't have much chance of taking down a full-grown giraffe. Giraffes can run up to 35 miles an hour (56 kph), and their lanky legs are actually quite powerful.

Are You a Giraffe?

IF YOU'RE ALWAYS LOOKING OUT FOR YOUR FRIENDS, YOU'VE GOT A LOT IN COMMON WITH THE GIRAFFE! THIS IS A GREAT ANIMAL FOR JAMMERS WHO ARE HELPFUL AND PRO-TECTIVE!

SAVANNAS
around the world

CHECK OUT OUR PLANET'S COOL GRASSLANDS!

GRASS AS FAR AS THE EYE can see! Grasslands are vast areas of land where grass makes up most of the plant life. Technically, a grassland is mostly made up of grasses from the Poaceae family or "true" grasses. It's one of the largest families of flowering plants, comprising around 10,000 species! This species variety gives the world's grasslands amazing diversity since it includes plants ranging from small wire grasses, bamboo, sugarcane, and even rice.

Chapada dos Veadeiros
National Park, Brazil

South America

Brazil's Cerrado, which is nearly three times the size of the state of Texas, U.S.A., is a savanna full of life. Endangered species like the maned wolf and giant anteater call this grassland home.

Bandhavgarh
National Park, India

Arctic Ocean

NORTH AMERICA
NORTH AMERICAN PRAIRIE
Pacific Ocean
Atlantic Ocean
SOUTH AMERICA
BRAZIL'S CERRADO

EUROPE
A S I A
AFRICA
INDIA'S TERAI-DUAR SAVANNA
Indian Ocean

Pacific Ocean
AUSTRALIA'S TROPICAL SAVANNA
AUSTRALIA

MAP KEY
☐ Featured Grassland
☐ Grassland

0   2000 miles
0   3000 kilometers

ANTARCTICA

Asia

The Terai-Duar savannas contain the highest concentrations of tigers and rhinos anywhere in the continent of Asia.

These prairies are places where the buffalo (also known as bison) roam, and the deer and the antelope play. You'll also find prairie dogs, coyotes, bobcats, wolves, and jackrabbits here.

Custer State Park,
South Dakota, U.S.A.

Mount Nameless,
Pilbara, Australia

Australia

Australia's tropical savanna is home to many animals, such as the kangaroo, and the dry season can last up to five months!

Spot the Differences

Safari Double Take

See if you can spot the 10 Differences Between these two pictures.

An elephant, a giraffe, and zebras visit a water hole in Africa.

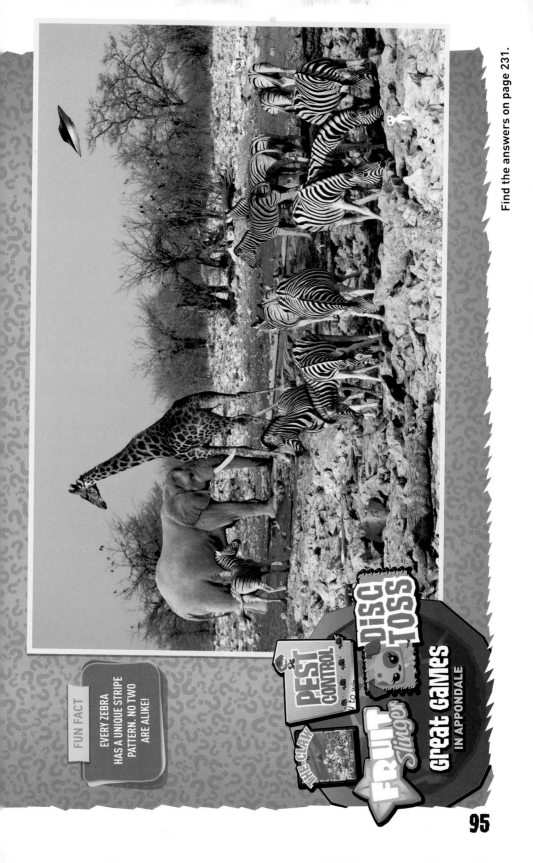

FUN FACT

EVERY ZEBRA HAS A UNIQUE STRIPE PATTERN. NO TWO ARE ALIKE!

Find the answers on page 231.

THE CLAW

FRUIT Slinger

PEST CONTROL

DISC TOSS

GREAT GAMES
IN APPONDALE

sarepia
FOREST

EXPLORE THE NETWORK OF BRIDGES that CONNECT THE TREES AND **FIND OUT WHAT SURPRISES** are IN THIS FOREST!

AS YOU ENTER THE QUIET AND DARK SAREPIA FOREST, you notice right away the giant trees looming high above. You take a deep breath of the fresh and crisp air before heading over to a ladder. As you climb high into the treetops, keep a lookout for birds that call the forest trees home. Once you get to the top, you can do some shopping at the Flag Shop, catch a movie at Sarepia Theater, or buy some cool plants for your den's garden.

Baby Bears: Brown bear cubs stay with Mom for two and a half years.

DESTINATION A.J.

SAREPIA THEATER

Follow the bright lights to the tree house theater nestled among the tops of Sarepia's giant trees! Before catching the show, grab some popcorn or stop by the photo booth to have your picture taken in the lobby. Fireflies glow softly inside the theater itself, where you can catch National Geographic Kids' movies about some of the weirdest and most fascinating animals in the world!

Once you're done exploring, ride the slide all the way to the forest floor—whee!

When you think of a forest, the first thing you think of is trees. There are a few different types of forests found all over the world and one thing they have in common is trees. But trees alone do not a forest make! The forest ecosystem consists of living things like plants, animals, and microorganisms as well as soil, water, climate, and rocks.

Fox Tails: Red foxes use their tails to help them balance!

The forest ecosystem is so important that even NASA examines it! You may be surprised to learn that the National Aeronautics and Space Administration doesn't only study faraway stars and planets, but also uses its high-tech imaging equipment to map and record the changes in the forests on Earth.

ALPHA TIP

Some animals in Jamaa, like the cheetah and the raccoon, come with exclusive colors that can't be chosen from the color menu!

Sir Gilbert

A biologist measures Hyperion, the tallest tree in the world.

Hikers walk through a redwood forest in California, U.S.A.

Redwood National Park
Where Giants Live

TOWERING TREE GIANTS SPAN THE redwood forests in California like leafy skyscrapers! Ancient redwood trees that thrive in the moist climate of the northern California coast can grow over 300 feet (90 m) tall and live for 2,000 years!

One by one these magnificent trees fell to loggers at the turn of the 20th century. To help protect the forests, 172-square-mile (445-sq-km) Redwood National Park was created in 1968. With its pleasant climate of mild winters and cool summers, hiking, backpacking, and camping are all popular activities. Between 1971 and 2009, more than 16 million people visited Redwood National Park.

The park is home to the tallest tree in the world, "Hyperion." It stands just over 379 feet (116 m)—three times the height of the Statue of Liberty, as measured from her heel to the top of her head. It might be tricky to go and see Hyperion in person, however. The hikers who found it and the scientists who measured it keep its location a secret to stop enthusiastic tourists from harming the tree.

Sea lions and harbor seals live off the park's coast, and gray whales can be seen as they migrate north from February to April. The Roosevelt elk can be seen year-round, along with black-tailed deer, foxes, bobcats, coyotes, and chipmunks. Visitors can also see black bears!

But in Sarepia Forest, Jammers can spot crazy creatures like crocodiles, elephants, lions, and even snow leopards year-round!

Heavyweights: Adult male Roosevelt elk can weigh over 875 pounds (397 kg).

SO YOU WANT TO BE A WOLF?

THEN THROW BACK YOUR HEAD AND HOWL!

GRAY WOLF

- ▸ **TYPE:** Mammal
- ▸ **DIET:** Ungulates (hooved animals like elk or bison), smaller mammals such as rodents, reptiles, and insects
- ▸ **LIFE SPAN:** 6 to 8 years
- ▸ **SIZE:** 4.5 to 6 feet (1.4 to 1.8 m) from head to tail
- ▸ **WEIGHT:** 50 to 110 pounds (22.7 to 50 kg)
- ▸ **STATUS:** Endangered
- ▸ **WHERE THEY LIVE:** North America, Asia, Europe

THAT'S HOW WOLVES COMMUNICATE IN THE WILD. They also talk to each other by whimpering, whining, growling, barking, yelping, and snarling.

Wolves are the largest members of the dog family. These canines are found all over the world, including Asia and the United States. The gray wolf is one of three species of wolf. The other two are the eastern wolf and the critically endangered red wolf. Subspecies of the gray wolf, like the Mexican gray wolf and the arctic wolf, exist around the world.

Wolves live in groups called packs and are great at teamwork. They work together to hunt, take care of young pups, and guard their land. So if you're a team player who doesn't mind babysitting your little brother or sister once in a while, you'll love being a wolf.

Are You a Wolf?

WOLVES ARE AVAILABLE TO ALL ANIMAL JAM PLAYERS. THERE'S ALSO A SPECIAL ARCTIC WOLF THAT MEMBERS CAN GET WITH A SPECIAL GIFT CARD. THIS IS A GREAT ANIMAL FOR ANIMAL JAM PLAYERS WHO ARE LOYAL AND PLAYFUL!

Wolf Play: Wolves and your pet dog are closely related. Wild wolves play together much like dogs do—wrestling, pouncing, and howling together.

Since wolf territories can range from 50 to 1,000 square miles (130 to 2,600 sq km) that means wolves sometimes have to go a long way to hunt their prey. When you're hungry, all you have to do is walk into your kitchen. Imagine having to search over 50 square miles (130 sq km) for a snack! It's no wonder that when wolves do find food, they gobble up so much of it. In one meal a wolf can eat about 20 pounds (9 kg) of meat. That would be like eating 80 hamburgers for lunch!

Comeback Pups: Gray wolves were hunted to near extinction all over the world. Now, populations are recovering.

Hero Trees

Helping People and the Planet

FORESTS COVER OVER 31 PERCENT OF THE total land area of the Earth and are an invaluable resource to both humans and animals. For humans, forests provide food, shelter, wood, paper, recreation, and provide 1.6 billion people around the world with their livelihoods. Worldwide, more than 300 million people call the forest home!

If biomes could be superheroes, forests would be among the first to get a cape! Trees produce oxygen; clean the air and soil of pollution; help fight flooding, wind erosion, and noise pollution; and keep us cool. Next time you see a tree you're probably going to want to run over and give it a great, big hug!

Liza

ALPHA TIP

Something magical will happen if a group of Jammers begin dancing next to the campfire in Sarepia Forest. The fire will grow larger and a mystical blue puff of smoke will slowly take shape. Keep dancing to see what—or who—it is!

Cool Gardens!

Plant lovers can get all their green needs, from flowers and plants to trees, at Treetop Gardens in Sarepia Forest. Turn your den into a forest with all the flower power you can find in this treetop store! Check out the following real-life incredible gardens and gadgets.

A Garden Fit for a King

One of the most famous gardens in the world is the garden at the palace of Versailles, France. Built in the 17th century, the garden has winding paths that lead to flower beds, statues, ornamental lakes, and the Grand Canal that King Louis XIV used for gondola rides!

Food Forest

The residents of Seattle, Washington, U.S.A., are thinking big when it comes to their community garden. They're building a huge food forest, or an edible park, where city dwellers can harvest fruits and veggies for their meals for free!

Mega Greenhouses

The greenhouses of Almería, Spain, are so tightly packed together they're visible from space! These greenhouses take up about 50,000 acres (20,000 ha) and produce tons of fruits and vegetables a year.

Poison Garden

Don't make a salad from this garden! The noble residents of Alnwick Castle in England, the site of Hogwarts in the Harry Potter movie series, grow a garden that includes deadly nightshade, hemlock, and other lethal plants.

THESE PLANTS CAN KILL

SO YOU WANT TO BE A DEER?

EXPLORE JAMAA IN LEAPS AND BOUNDS!

GRACEFUL AND BEAUTIFUL deer are found around the world in forests, tundra, and grasslands. There are 47 different types of deer species including elk, caribou, and reindeer. The biggest member of the deer family is the moose, which weighs in at 1,800 pounds (816 kg).

One thing most deer have in common are their antlers —worn mostly by males. The only species that doesn't have antlers is the Chinese water deer. Instead, they have fanglike tusks that protrude from their mouths!

Although some species of deer are endangered, most are thriving. In the United States and Canada, deer have even become a bit of a nuisance in suburbs and cities by showing up uninvited to dine in people's gardens!

Are You a Deer?

KNOWN FOR ITS SPEED AND AGILITY, THE DEER IS A GREAT ANIMAL FOR JAMMERS WHO ARE QUICK AND NIMBLE!

Speedsters: White-tailed deer can sprint up to 30 miles an hour (48 kph) and leap as far as 30 feet (9 m) in a single bound!

STATS

WHITE-TAILED DEER

▶ **TYPE:** Mammal
▶ **DIET:** Grass, leaves, twigs, fruits, nuts, corn, alfalfa, lichens and other fungi
▶ **LIFE SPAN:** Up to 10 years
▶ **SIZE:** 6 to 7.75 feet (1.8 to 2.4 m)
▶ **WEIGHT:** 110 to 300 pounds (50 to 136 kg)
▶ **WHERE THEY LIVE:** North America and South America

104

Life Up Top: Raccoons like to build their dens high above ground. They're often found at the tops of houses or buildings.

...or a RACCOON?

PUT ON A MASK AND GET READY TO PLAY!

THESE NOCTURNAL animals are most active at night. So if you're the last one to nod off at a sleepover party, you've got a lot in common with this mammal. There are seven species of raccoon, the most common being the northern raccoon. Raccoons live throughout much of the world, from North and South America to Asia. In fact, these mammals can live in many different environments. They're known for being just as at home in the wilderness as they are in your backyard or in a big city.

STATS

NORTHERN RACCOON

▸ **TYPE:** Mammal
▸ **DIET:** Fruits, seeds, nuts, birds' eggs, fish, frogs, crayfish, and plants
▸ **LIFE SPAN:** 5 years
▸ **SIZE:** 30 to 36 inches (75 to 91 cm) from head to tail
▸ **WEIGHT:** 22 to 44 pounds (10 to 20 kg)
▸ **WHERE THEY LIVE:** Canada, United States, and Central America

Are You a Raccoon?

LOVE TO STAY UP LATE? YOU'LL LOVE BEING A RACCOON! THIS IS A GREAT ANIMAL FOR JAMMERS WHO ARE MISCHIEVOUS NIGHT OWLS.

Forests
around the world

FORESTS COME IN ALL SIZES and types and can be found throughout the world—even in the ocean! Forests are classified by their latitude, or their distance from the Equator. But under the waves, there's another type of forest, too! All forests are home to millions of creatures big and small!

Tropical Forests

These types of forests occur near the Equator and are home to over half of the world's plant and animal species. There's no winter in a tropical forest. The average temperature is a mild 68° to 77° Fahrenheit (20° to 25°C), so leave the snow boots at home when visiting here!

Arctic Ocean

NORTH AMERICA

EUROPE

A S I A

Pacific Ocean

Atlantic Ocean

AFRICA

Pacific Ocean

SOUTH AMERICA

Indian Ocean

0   2000 miles
0   3000 kilometers

AUSTRALIA

MAP KEY
- Boreal Forest
- Kelp Forest
- Temperate Forest
- Tropical Forest

ANTARCTICA

Boreal Forests

Located the farthest from the Equator are boreal, or taiga, forests. The cold, harsh climate in this biome makes life for animals tough. To survive the winter, many animals hibernate or migrate to somewhere warmer. Boreal forests can be found in North America and parts of Russia and Scandinavia.

Temperate Forests

Unlike in tropical forests, the seasons do change in temperate forests located in eastern North America, parts of Russia, China, and Japan, and Western Europe. The trees lose their leaves after they turn color, from green to autumnal, in the fall. Then, trees regrow their foliage in the spring.

Kelp Forests

Kelp forests can be found in cold ocean waters and provide food and shelter for marine life. Kelp is one of the fastest growing plants in the world!

107

THE Tree Giants

MEET THE SEQUOIA AND THE REDWOOD

TWO KINDS OF TREE TAKE THE PRIZE for being the biggest on Earth: redwoods and sequoias, which live on the west coast of the United States.

Redwood trees are strong and sturdy. Their bark can be up to one foot (30 cm) thick and fire resistant, protecting the trees from forest fires. Some trees that have been scorched in wildfires are still alive and growing!

Giant sequoias are a species of redwood that boasts the largest tree in the world in terms of volume, or how much wood it has. Redwoods grow to be the world's tallest trees, but have a more slender trunk. But both are supertrees that provide a home for hundreds of plants and animals.

Sequoia National Park

An Ancient Refuge

FIND OUT WHAT IT FEELS LIKE TO BE AN ant or another tiny creature by visiting Sequoia National Park. When you stand next to the ancient, towering sequoia trees you'll feel like a bug!

The park was formed in 1890 to protect the world's largest and oldest living things: giant sequoias! While Redwood National Park is home to the tallest tree, Sequoia National Park is home to the largest tree, the General Sherman Tree. Measured by how much wood the trunk alone has, which is called wood volume, the massive sequoia is estimated at slightly over 52,500 cubic feet (1,486.6 m³).

Neighboring Kings Canyon National Park is operated jointly with Sequoia National Park. Massive mountains and trees tower above the landscape, and seemingly bottomless canyons and caves are carved deep into the ground. Mount Whitney, the highest peak in the United States south of Alaska, rises to 14,491 feet (4,417 m) here.

Visitors at the parks who observe any of the diverse wildlife that lives here—gray fox, black bear, mule deer, bighorn sheep, kingsnakes, or California newts—can stop by the visitor center and have their find entered into the park's database of wildlife sightings. Just like a real-life Journey Book!

Standing Watch: Sentinel, a 700-ton (635-MT) sequoia, grows right outside the Giant Forest Museum in the national park.

Forest DoubleTake

See if you can spot the 10 differences between these two pictures.

Colorful autumn leaves make for a bright walk through the woods.

FUN FACT

A BROWN BEAR CAN LOSE HUNDREDS OF POUNDS (KG) WHEN IT HIBERNATES— THAT'S LIKE LOSING THE WEIGHT OF A WASHING MACHINE!

DEAD END

Wind Rider

THE CLAW

SUPER SORT

HIDE N HIDE

BILE BUDE

Great Games
IN SAREPIA FOREST

Find the answers on page 231.

CORAL CANYONS

WALK ALONG THE ROCKY DESERT TRAILS AS YOU ADMIRE THE RED ROCK MESAS IN THIS BEAUTIFUL DESERT LAND!

EAGLES SOAR HIGH ABOVE YOU AS YOU DECIDE WHAT TO do here first. Should you dress your best for the chance to win Gems in Best Dressed? Or stop off at the Art Studio to create something amazing? In Coral Canyons, you can do that and more!

While deserts aren't barren, the idea of them as very dry is true. An area classified as a desert gets less than 10 inches (25 cm) of precipitation a year. It also has to lose more water through evaporation than it receives through rainfall.

DESTINATION A.J.

EPIC WONDERS

Escape the heat of the Coral Canyons desert and step inside a cool cave of mystery: Epic Wonders. The entrance to this grand shop is hidden behind a waterfall that flows over the mesa.

There's something magical about this place. Mystical music plays as floating orbs dance in the air. A treasure trove of golden bricks is piled on the floor, letting you know that this shop is something special.

At Epic Wonders you can buy dazzling crystal statues of the Alphas, rare birthstones, and epic den items you can't find anywhere else. The orb at the top of the stone staircase offers legendary clothing items, which can totally transform your look!

Don't let the harsh climate fool you. Deserts are biologically rich habitats teeming with animals and plants! It's not easy, but the trick to living in the dry desert is to adapt to a life with very little water. It's something the creatures of the desert have perfected in order to survive.

Your animal may not feel the heat in Jamaa, but check out the cool animal adaptations of real-life creatures as you collect them in your Journey Book!

DESERT MYSTERIES

Fairy Circles

For a long time these mysterious circles in Africa were believed to be the footprints of gods or caused by dancing fairies. Biologists now think sand termites are the real cause!

Moving Rocks

Rocks in Death Valley, California, U.S.A., have mysteriously traveled distances of up to half a mile (0.8 km)! No one has seen them move, but they leave long tracks etched in the sand. Scientists think the cause could be found in the winter, when enough water and ice could potentially form to float the rocks.

UFOs in Roswell

In 1947, a strange object crashed into the desert outside Roswell, New Mexico, U.S.A. Although the government denies it, people to this day believe it was a flying saucer, or a UFO, complete with an alien crew!

A fennec fox's big ears help it stay cool.

Sand dunes are formed by the wind in the Sahara.

IN NORTHERN AFRICA, A SEEMingly endless sea of sand extends 3,320,000 square miles (8,600,000 sq km). This place is the Sahara, the largest hot desert in the world!

With temperatures reaching 122°F (50°C) during the hottest months, the Sahara is not a very hospitable place. Yet animals like snakes, rodents, and scorpions thrive in these extreme conditions. Gazelles, deer, baboons, hyenas, and foxes also have what it takes to tough it out in the Sahara. Lions roam the southernmost section of this desert. The lakes and pools of the Sahara are inhabited by crocodiles, frogs, and toads.

There's not a lot of Saharan vegetation, but the few grasses, herbs, shrubs, and trees that live here are heat and drought tolerant. They have to be in order to make it in this dangerous climate!

Even people manage to live here. Cities and villages are built around oases, small patches of vegetation surrounded by desert. But most people of the Sahara are in fact nomads, who live their lives moving throughout this desert landscape. The Valley of Whales is an area of the Sahara believed to have been the home of an ancient sea 37 million years ago. Today it contains an amazing collection of fossils unlike any other in the world: whales with legs! Basilosaurus fossils have two tiny legs that scientists believe prove modern-day whales descended from land mammals that once walked on all fours. These fossils, along with shark teeth, sea urchin spines, and the bones of giant catfish, can be seen all throughout this great valley.

Dry as Bone: Fossilized bones of ancient whales are scattered throughout parts of the Sahara, such as these in western Egypt.

COLD deserts

Get out your parka and earmuffs!

IT'S HARD TO IMAGINE, BUT COLD deserts really do exist. In fact, they are the largest deserts in the world!

While the Sahara is the world's largest hot desert, the biggest desert in the world is a polar desert. The Antarctic desert stretches over 5.5 million square miles (14.2 million sq km) around the South Pole. But, where's the sand? And the heat? Remember, a desert is defined by the amount of precipitation it receives each year, not by sand or temperature. The icy floors of the Antarctic desert are made up of ice that has been there for a very long time, not from newly fallen snow or rain. Instead of being hot and dry, polar deserts are cold and dry.

The second largest polar desert is found at the North Pole and spans over the United States, Canada, Finland, Greenland, Iceland, Norway, Sweden, and Russia.

GRAHAM

ALPHA TIP

Is the stone bridge in Coral Canyons structurally sound? When three or more Jammers jump on it, it cracks. But no matter how many Jammers pile on and start hopping, the bridge has not broken—yet. I wonder what will happen when it does . . .

ART STUDIO

Take a break from Coral Canyon's desert sun and create some artwork at the Art Studio! This colorful artist's studio is tucked into the mesa rocks of the landscape. It's rumored to be a favorite place of Peck, the artistic Alpha. Choose from several activities to create your own masterpiece.

At the table near the door you can print out pictures of animals to color, as well as fun word games to play. Or take a turn on the pottery wheel and print out pictures of beautiful pieces of pottery to color.

Unleash your inner Picasso with the painting activity at the artist's easel. Choose your colors, tools, and shapes to create a work of art. Print out the artwork when you're finished to show it off to your family and friends. Or submit it to Animal Jam HQ. You just might see it featured in the gallery on Jammer Central!

FUN FACT

PEOPLE HAVE BEEN CELEBRATING THEIR RELATIONSHIP WITH NATURE THROUGH ART FOR AROUND 20,000 YEARS! THE ANCIENT CAVE PAINTINGS OF LASCAUX CAVE IN FRANCE FEATURE STAGS, BULLS, CATTLE, BISON, FELINES, AND EVEN A BIRD, A BEAR, AND A RHINOCEROS!

Desert STORMS

WATCH OUT FOR THAT DUST!

AS THE DESERT SURFACE HEATS UP, it kicks up a devil of a storm: a dust devil! When patches of ground sizzle under the desert sun, it causes the heated air near the surface to rise and spin. A spinning cylinder of hot air forms. As it travels, it picks up loose objects from the earth like dirt, leaves, and dust. Resembling tiny tornadoes, these whirlwinds of air and debris can rise hundreds of feet into the air!

Dust devils around the world have been associated with legends of evil spirits. In Africa they're thought to be demons, while in Australia parents tell their children the dust devils are spirits who will whisk them away if they are naughty! In the southwestern United States, they get their name for being, well, devilish.

DESTINATION A.J.

DEN SHOP

One of the stone staircases in Coral Canyons leads to the Den Shop. Here you can get an all-new den with cool choices from a Fantasy Castle to a Sunken Ship!

SO YOU WANT TO BE A FOX?

TWITCH YOUR TAIL!

ADAPTABLE FOXES LIVE ALL OVER the world and can be found in habitats ranging from forests, grasslands, mountains, and deserts.

Sly foxes are related to dogs, wolves, and coyotes. Fox species include the North American gray fox, red fox, South American fox, the arctic fox, the bat-eared fox, and the crab-eating fox.

When faced with a predator, the crafty fox knows it won't win in a fight. Instead, it will try to outsmart its opponent so it can get away. This resourcefulness has earned the fox a reputation for intelligence.

Diverse Diet
Foxes eat mice, rabbits, fruit, eggs, birds, domesticated poultry, pet food, and even garbage.

STATS

RED FOX

- **TYPE:** Mammal
- **DIET:** Small animals, fruit, vegetables, and fish
- **LIFE SPAN:** 2 to 4 years
- **SIZE:** 30 to 55.5 inches (76 to 141 cm) from head to tail
- **WEIGHT:** 6.5 to 24 pounds (3 to 11 kg)
- **WHERE THEY LIVE:** Europe, Asia, Africa, North America, and Australia

Are You a Fox?

FOXES THINK FAST ON THEIR FEET! KNOWN FOR THEIR ADAPTABILITY AND ABILITY TO GET OUT OF A JAM, THIS IS A GREAT ANIMAL FOR SMART, SLY JAMMERS!

Water in the Desert

LOOKING DEEP UNDERGROUND FOR PRECIOUS WATER

WATER IS CRUCIAL FOR survival—especially for humans! You can live for up to three days without water. After that, you'll perish! So how do people build cities in the arid desert?

Savvy desert dwellers search for groundwater below the surface of the sand in aquifers. When it rains, snows, or hails, the precipitation seeps into the ground. It can remain there for thousands of years. People in deserts often drill into the ground for this valuable resource. Aquifers are used in desert cities around the globe, including the American Southwest and the Middle East, to fulfill water needs. In the Negev, a desert in Israel, aquifers provide water for crops and even fish farming!

A long, winding road slithers across the Gobi desertscape.

Nomadic Life: Mongolian tribes use Bactrian camels to carry goods in the Gobi.

The Gobi
Waterless Place

ALTHOUGH THE GOBI DOES have areas of sand, much of it is covered in rocks! And for some—treasure!

Located in northern China and Mongolia, the Gobi takes up a total area of 500,000 square miles (1,300,000 sq km), making it the fourth largest desert in the world. The Mongolian people named it Gobi, which means "waterless place." Like all deserts, the Gobi receives very little rainfall per year. In fact, parts of this desert are completely waterless.

There's not a lot of vegetation in this dry climate but wild camels, gazelles, and antelope roam the land. Reptiles and rodents also call the Gobi home. Very few people live in this desert and those who do are nomads who raise cattle and other livestock on the land.

Now back to that treasure! Water may be scarce, but one thing the Gobi is not lacking is fossils. In fact, a certain stretch of this desert holds a treasure trove of dinosaur and early mammal remains from the Cretaceous period, over 80 million years ago. Paleontologists flock to the Gobi to hunt for these rare and incredible fossil riches. The Gobi has yielded never-before-known dinosaur species, new insights into how dinosaurs lived, and dinosaur eggs complete with intact, fossilized embryos, or unhatched baby dinosaurs. Paleontologists believe they have only scratched the surface of this amazing desert land and that many more exciting finds are waiting to be discovered!

FUN FACT

A TEAM OF SEVEN PEOPLE WALKED 1,000 MILES (1,610 KM) ACROSS THE GOBI IN 51 DAYS, 11 HOURS, AND 40 MINUTES, IN TEMPERATURES AS HIGH AS 104°F (40°C)!

121

SO YOU WANT TO BE a LION?

IT STARTS OFF AS A LOW growl. The hairs on the back of your neck stand up as the growl gets louder, turning into a ferocious roar! The roar of a male lion can be heard up to 5 miles (8 km) away. Despite their blood-curdling cries, lions live together in close family groups called prides. Prides consist of about a dozen females, cubs, and usually only two to three males. Male lions sometimes get a bad rap. They're labeled as lazy because the females in the pride do most of the hunting and parenting. But the male lion has an important job: protecting the pride's territory. He roams areas of grasslands that can be as large as 100 square miles (259 sq km) to scare away any animals that intrude on the pride's land.

Strong Survivors: Kalahari Desert lions have learned to go without drinking water for weeks.

Let out your Wildest Roar!

Are You a Lion?

BE THE KING—OR QUEEN—OF THE JUNGLE WHEN YOU CHOOSE THIS AWESOME ANIMAL. THIS IS A GREAT ANIMAL FOR JAMMERS WHO ARE LOUD AND STRONG!

STATS

AFRICAN LION

- **TYPE:** Mammal
- **DIET:** Gazelles, zebras, impalas, wildebeests, and smaller animals such as birds, rodents, and fish
- **LIFE SPAN:** Up to 18 years
- **SIZE:** Head and body, 4.5 to 6.5 feet (1.4 to 2 m); tail, 26.3 to 39.5 inches (67 to 100 cm)
- **WEIGHT:** 265 to 420 pounds (120 to 191 kg)
- **STATUS:** Vulnerable
- **WHERE THEY LIVE:** Africa

122

...or a HORSE?

GALLOP TO YOUR HEART'S CONTENT!

Running Free: Mustang horses roam freely on the plains of the American West.

FROM AFAR, THE SOUND OF thundering hoofbeats reaches your ears . . . and then, suddenly, a herd of mustangs comes galloping into view! Mustangs are fast, graceful, and powerful free-roaming horses. Even though mustangs roam freely, they are not technically wild horses. In fact, they are thought to be descended from Spanish Iberian horses, and were first brought to the United States by Spanish explorers in the 1500s. In later years, mustangs became the main transportation of cowboys, ranchers, and pioneers. Today, they live in the western part of the United States, where they graze on open plains and travel in large herds led by a female horse (called a mare). Mustangs are slightly smaller and lighter than the average horse, and are known for their speed, agility, and intelligence.

STATS

MUSTANG HORSE

- ▶ TYPE: Mammal
- ▶ DIET: Perennial grasses
- ▶ LIFE SPAN: Up to 20 years
- ▶ SIZE: 4.8 to 5 feet at the shoulder (1.3 to 1.5 m)
- ▶ WEIGHT: 750 to 2,200 pounds (340 to 454 kg)
- ▶ WHERE THEY LIVE: Western United States

123

LIVING IN EXTREMES

Clever animals have come up with many ways to beat the heat and find and hold on to water while living in the harsh desert. It's not easy living in a desert biome, but these animals make it work!

Gila monster

Shun the Sun To escape the sun, some desert animals like rodents and foxes are nocturnal and primarily come out at night. Rattlesnakes and Gila monsters are crepuscular, meaning they are only active during dawn or dusk.

Fennec fox

Self-Cooling The long ears, legs, and tails of certain desert mammals help them to expel body heat. Dark colors absorb light and trap heat; so to soak up less sun many desert animals are light colored.

Turkey vulture

Air-Conditioning Nature's Way When desert birds like vultures urinate on their legs and feet, it's called urohydrosis, a unique way of cooling off the blood circulated through the bird's body. What a weird form of air-conditioning!

Cougar

Water Works Predators like hawks, lions, eagles, and coyotes get their moisture from the blood and water in their prey. Some animals will look for moist soil by burrowing deep underground and absorbing the water found there through their skin.

Grand Canyon
History in Stone

THE NATURAL wonders of the Grand Canyon National Park draw approximately five million visitors each year. That's a lot of people, and they're all there to see a lot of rock: 277 miles (445 km) long, about a mile (1.6 km) deep, and 18 miles (29 km) wide of it! It's no wonder Jamaa's Coral Canyons is based on this cool real-life place!

Located in Arizona, U.S.A., the Grand Canyon lies in the Colorado Plateau. Millions of years of erosion by the Colorado River created the spectacular canyon.

Desert Life

LIVING THINGS BEAT THE HEAT!

A CARPET OF BRIGHTLY COLORED WILDFLOWERS STRETCHES in front of you, their fragrant scent filling the air. You're not in a lush meadow, but a desert. How is it possible? To survive in this dry land, desert plants have to learn how to adapt to a life with little water and temperature extremes.

Xerophytes, like cacti, are able to store water in times of droughts. Other types of desert plants, phreatophytes, search out water deep underground by growing extremely long roots.

The yearly explosion of desert wildflowers happens after a seasonal rainy period. The seeds of these flowers lay dormant under the sandy soil until the rains bring them to vibrant life!

Tourists look out into the Grand Canyon from a glass-floored skywalk.

Exposed rock layers from the canyon's walls offer valuable information to geologists about the history of our planet. Some of the rocks are as old as 1.8 billion years!

People have been living in the Grand Canyon for a long time, too. Human artifacts dating nearly 12,000 years old have been found here. Scientists have even discovered archaeological remains from a dozen different kinds of culture groups, including Zuni, Hopi, and Navajo.

The Hualapai Tribe continues to live here on a reservation, and they manage the Skywalk, a glass floor projecting about 70 feet (21 m) over the canyon, from which brave visitors can enjoy the view.

Diverse habitats, from mountain forests to deserts, can be found in the Grand Canyon. This varied landscape means that a wide variety of wildlife calls the Grand Canyon home, including the California condor, bald and golden eagles, mountain lions, bighorn sheep, coyotes, and the deadly black widow spider.

It's no wonder this amazing place is considered one of the natural wonders of the world!

HAPPENING HABITATS

These facts appear throughout the book. See if you know the answers to these trivia questions.

#1 What is the largest hot desert in the world?

a. Sonoran Desert
b. The Gobi
c. The Sahara
d. Kalahari Desert

#2 Tropical rain forests are home to what percentage of the world's plant and animal species?

a. About 50%
b. 3%
c. 22%
d. 98%

#3 Oceans cover 71 percent of the Earth's surface.

True or False?

#4 During the Great Migration, over a million wildebeests travel every season through this biome:

a. Amazon rain forest
b. Serengeti savanna
c. The Gobi
d. Arctic tundra

#5 Sunlight can't reach the ocean floor in the majority of the ocean.

True or False?

#8 A habitat or biome is:

a. An endangered species of monkey
b. The world's oldest mountain range
c. Another name for a seagull's nest
d. A region and climate where a community of plants and animals live

#6 Desert plants classified as xerophytes search out water by growing really long roots deep underground.

True or False?

#9 Which of the following habitats receives little to no rain each year?

a. Rain forest
b. Desert
c. Temperate forest
d. Savanna

#10 Which habitat does a sloth live in?

a. Ocean
b. Pond
c. Rain forest
d. Desert

#7 The most lethal animal in the world can be found where?

a. The Outback
b. The Amazon rain forest
c. The Serengeti
d. The Great Barrier Reef

SKY HIGH

Sssssnake!

Long Shot

BEST DRESSED

EAGLE

GREAT GAMES IN CORAL CANYONS

CRYSTAL SANDS

THE SUN IS ALWAYS SHINING HERE!
RELAX WHILE THE MELLOW SOUNDS OF THE OCEAN'S WAVES FILL THE AIR.

IT'S UP TO YOU IF YOU WANT TO KEEP THE LAID-BACK vibe going or if you want to play! Curl up on one of the towels on the sandy beach, have fun in the crystal clear waters, or take a ride down one of the waterslides for a splashing good time. Crystal Sands is not just a relaxation getaway, but also the gateway to Jamaa's oceans. Walk down the dock or jump in from Tierney's Aquarium to start exploring the water.

Tierney's
Aquarium

129

TIERNEY'S AQUARIUM

On the sunny beaches of Crystal Sands you'll find National Geographic explorer and marine biologist Dr. Tierney Thys's aquarium. Tierney has traveled all over the world to study ocean life. She loves her work so much she wanted to share the wonders of the oceans with Jammers by setting up an aquarium in Jamaa!

Experience what it's like to be a marine biologist. Check out Tierney's tech bench with tools like underwater cameras, scooters, shark suits, and more.

Watch the fish swim by in the aquarium exhibits, or get up close and personal with marine life like rays, hermit crabs, and sea stars in the Touch Pool. Fill in the log to win cool prizes! You can also print out ocean life puzzles and pictures here.

All over the world, beaches are popular vacation destinations. They are a perfect place to relax in the sun or take part in fun activities like swimming, surfing, snorkeling, kayaking, and more! So many people enjoy beaches. But how many know exactly what a beach is?

Colorful Dives: There's so much to discover beneath the waves as the diver (top) finds on this Dominican Republic reef. A colorful bat star and orange cup corals brighten the seafloor off southern California, U.S.A. (above).

The area of land that lies next to an ocean, lake, or river is called a coast, or shore. Beaches are formed when waves carry crushed seashells, sand, and gravel to the shore and deposit them there. Over time, these washed-up pieces of organic matter accumulate, making the beach you spread your towel and build your sand castles on!

Beach Treasure: Sand is made of finely crushed seashells. But shells, rocks, and more can be found on beaches!

ALPHA TIP

Liza

While you are using the Cotton Candy Machine at the Summer Carnival, choose the black flavor, then the white flavor, and then the black flavor again to make a Phantom treat!

STRIKE A POSE! THE pale pink sands, cerulean waters, and leafy palm trees found on Anse Source d'Argent beach have made it one of the most photographed beaches in the world! This gorgeous tropical beach can be found in Seychelles, an island republic in the western Indian Ocean that's located about 1,000 miles (1,609 km) east of Kenya and 700 miles (1,127 km) northeast of Madagascar.

The Seychelles are made up of 115 islands, and though it's one of the world's smallest countries, it's home to a wide variety of marine life and lush vegetation. Jellyfish trees and the rare coco de mer plants—whose seeds weigh 66 pounds (30 kg), the largest in the plant kingdom—are among the 200 plant species on the islands. Divers can explore the turquoise waters that are home to more than 900 kinds of fish!

The three main islands of Seychelles are Praslin, La Digue, and Mahé, and all are popular tourist destinations. The Anse Source d'Argent beach is known for its coral sand surrounded by granite boulders. A reef shelters the water, protecting the beach from receiving too much wave action, making the Anse Source d'Argent surf calm, shallow, and very relaxing. There are many other beaches in the Seychelles island chain where visitors can swim, snorkel, and surf. They all feature soft sand and crystal clear warm water, a perfect vacation combination.

Anse Source d'Argent at Seychelles appears in many tropical beach photos.

Seychelles Beaches

Tropical Paradise

Seychelles giant tortoise

DESTINATION A.J.

TIERNEY'S THEATER

Head upstairs to the aquarium's theater to relax on a beach towel while watching Tierney answer Jammers' questions about animals. If you've been wondering about ocean life, this is where you can ask her a question of your own!

SO YOU WANT TO BE A DOLPHIN?

FLIP FOR FUN IN JAMAA!

DOLPHINS HAVE FINS AND spend their whole lives underwater, but don't confuse them with fish! Dolphins are mammals who are warm-blooded, nurse their young with milk, and have lungs, just like humans. To breathe, dolphins must go to the surface of the water periodically to take in air through a blowhole on the top of their body. Dolphins are supersmart and social, so they make lots of noise when communicating with each other using moans, groans, squeaks, whistles, and grunts!

Dolphins can be found in every ocean in the world, and even in some rivers. Dolphins are considered to be toothed whales. There are about 40 species of dolphins, and 6 of those are commonly called whales although they are really dolphins. In fact, the orca, or killer whale, is the largest species of dolphin!

Sea Smarties: Scientists use whistles and hand signals to communicate directly with intelligent and playful bottlenose dolphins.

STATS

BOTTLENOSE DOLPHIN

▸ **TYPE:** Mammal
▸ **DIET:** Fish, shrimp, and squid
▸ **LIFE SPAN:** 45 to 50 years
▸ **SIZE:** 10 to 14 feet (3 to 4.2 m)
▸ **WEIGHT:** 1,100 pounds (500 kg)
▸ **WHERE THEY LIVE:** Harbors, bays, gulfs, and estuaries in mostly temperate and tropical waters

...or a
PENGUIN?
PUT a LittLe WaDDLe iN your walk!

THE PENGUINS' SHORT LEGS and squat bodies give them their signature walk. Penguins can't fly in the sky but they sure can "fly" underwater! They propel themselves at high speeds when swimming and will leap out of the water from time to time to breathe. The fairy penguin is the smallest of the 18 penguin species and stands only 14 inches (35 cm) tall, while the Emperor penguin towers above it at a height of 45 inches (115 cm), making it the largest of the species. You may think that all penguins live in cold climates, but African penguins are found off the coast of southern Africa. They search out the cooler waters of the Benguela Current to hunt in. African penguins make a loud braying sound similar to a donkey.

STATS

AFRICAN PENGUIN

▸ TYPE: Bird
▸ DIET: Sardines, anchovies, and squid
▸ LIFE SPAN: 10 to 15 years
▸ SIZE: 17.7 inches (45 cm)
▸ WEIGHT: 6.83 pounds (3.1 kg)
▸ STATUS: Endangered
▸ WHERE THEY LIVE: Along the coast of Namibia and South Africa

Are You a Penguin?

ADORABLE AND QUICK, PENGUINS ARE PERFECT ANIMALS FOR JAMMERS WHO ARE SPEEDY AND WOULDN'T MIND LIVING WITH ALL THEIR FRIENDS!

133

COLORFUL BEACHES!

SANDY BEACHES are MANY DIFFERENT COLORS!

WHEN YOU TRUDGE TOWARD THE WATER, loaded down with chairs, umbrellas, sand toys, and picnic baskets, the sand you are camping out on could be pink or even black, depending on what part of the world you are in!

Sandy beaches come in many different colors. Coral beaches are made from the eroded exoskeletons of coral and are usually white and powdery, especially in the Caribbean Sea. Some even have pink sand! The black beach berms are found on volcanic islands, including Hawaii, U.S.A. When lava flows into the ocean, it eventually cools, then explodes into thousands of tiny fragments, creating jet-black beaches.

Seeing Pink: Some of the world's pink beaches get their special hue from a type of red marine plankton called foraminifera. It mixes with white sand to look pink!

DESTINATION A.J.

CAPTAIN MELVILLE'S JUICE HUT

All that swimming and playing on the beach can make an animal thirsty! Refresh yourself at Captain Melville's Juice Hut with your choice of delicious fruit smoothies. Look for the straw hut in Crystal Sands for this cool place to escape the sun. Try your luck at The Claw machine, or hop on the stage and sing a song for your fellow Jammers.

PET WASH

Stinky pet? Clean him up at the Pet Wash! Follow the rocky path up from Tierney's Aquarium to have a splashing good time with your pet.

What's Underneath the Sand?

On the beach, many creatures live their lives among the grains of sand you're standing on. Some you can see, while you'd need a microscope to know the others were there!

Beach Hoppers

Tiny holes around washed-up piles of seaweed mean beach hoppers! At night, you can see these critters hopping on the sand as they search for food.

Coquina Clams

These colorful mollusks live in the top inch (2.5 cm) of sand and use the waves to move up and down the beach.

Bloodworms

These wiggly beach worms get their name from their red color. These worms can grow over 14 inches (37 cm) long!

Sand Crabs

By scooting backward, these cute crabs bury themselves in the wet sand but leave their antennae poking out.

Sand Creatures You Can't See

That bucket of sand you're using to build your sand castle? It's alive! Thousands of tiny creatures are living in it. One of them is the water bear, or tardigrade, and it's less than one millimeter long.

HELP KEEP OUR BEACHES CLEAN!

REDUCING POLLUTION AND TRASH

IMAGINE IF THE home you lived in was filled with toxic chemicals, sewage, and garbage. Unfortunately, many marine animals have to live in these conditions. Beach pollution is harmful to wildlife and humans, but you can help put a stop to it!

When you're visiting the beach, make sure to throw out your garbage in trash cans at the beach or take it home with you. Things you don't dispose of properly at home, even if you live many miles from the ocean, can still end up there. Garbage presents a choking hazard to birds and dolphins, and sea lions can get tangled up in twine, ropes, or other debris. Reducing pollution is the best way to keep our beaches healthy!

Durdle Door beach has a famous rock arch extending into the sea.

TAKING A WALK ON THE BEACHES here is more like traveling in a time machine through the Triassic, Jurassic, and Cretaceous periods! This 95-mile (153-km) stretch on the south coast of England features rocky shores, beaches, cliffs, and 185 million years of geological history. It's called Jurassic Coast, and it's brimming with fossils.

The initial fossil find was in 1811, when a 12-year-old girl named Mary Anning and her brother discovered the first complete *Ichthyosaurus* fossil. Since then, fossil hunters have flocked to the site. Mary even became one when she grew up!

Even though scientists have poured over Jurassic Coast ever since Mary's find, there are still plenty of new discoveries waiting to be found. The winter weather chips away at the fossil layers each year to reveal more hidden treasures. One of the most exciting was the skull of a giant sea monster that could have eaten a *Tyrannosaurus rex* as a snack! The 12-ton (11-MT), ferocious pliosaur lived 150 million years ago.

Fossil hunting is easy on the Jurassic Coast. Fossils can be found right out in the open, lying on the ground.

Dino Coast: The coastal cliffs of Jurassic Coast are famous for fossil collecting.

Collecting them is permitted in some areas, like the beach at Charmouth. Fossils that have fallen from the overhead cliffs are considered abandoned and are up for grabs! But don't show up with a chisel and hammer to pry fossils out of the rock formations on the coast. That would be breaking the law.

SO YOU WANT TO BE A SEAL?

MAKE A SPLASH!

JUST EXPECT YOUR DIP IN THE ocean to be on the chilly side. Most of the 33 species of seals live their lives in cold waters. But the cold is no problem when you've got a built-in wet suit in the form of a thick layer of blubber!

Seals are broken into two groups: earless—or true—seals, and eared seals. These mammals are found all over the world, although they are more common in polar seas. Some species are found in the open ocean, while others like to live near islands, shores, or ice floes.

Are You a Seal?

FOR JAMMERS WHO ARE FRIENDLY AND LOVE TO SWIM! STAY UNDER THE SEA ALL YOU LIKE BECAUSE AS A SEAL YOU CAN HOLD YOUR BREATH BENEATH THE WAVES OF JAMAA FOR AS LONG AS YOU'D LIKE TO EXPLORE!

HARP SEAL

▸ **TYPE:** Mammal
▸ **DIET:** Arctic cod, herring, and capelin fish
▸ **LIFE SPAN:** 30 years
▸ **SIZE:** 6.25 feet (1.9 m) long
▸ **WEIGHT:** 265 to 300 pounds (120 to 136 kg)
▸ **STATUS:** Least concern
▸ **WHERE THEY LIVE:** North Atlantic and Arctic Oceans

Deep Diver: To hunt for fish and crustaceans, harp seals will dive anywhere from 300 feet (90 m) to nearly 1,000 feet (300 m).

IN THE FIELD WITH TIERNEY THYS

HARP SEALS GROW UP

The name harp seal comes from the large, harp-shaped ring on the seal's back. But harp seals aren't born with this marking. In fact, baby harp seals, or pups, are famous for their beautiful, pure white coats.

The pups shed their white coats after three weeks' time. When they are born, the pups don't have any blubber. But Mom's high-fat milk helps them to pack on the pounds quickly! When the pups reach about 80 pounds (36 kg), their mothers stop nursing them. They can lose about half of their body weight by the time they learn to dive into the sea to hunt for themselves.

WHO WORE it BEST?

IN JAMAA, WHO WEARS IT BEST ON THE BEACH? Everyone! With tons of fun clothing and accessories to choose from, you'll always be best dressed. Check out how these seals and deer make sunny accessories look like a breeze. Which do you like the best?

All eyes will be on you in this cute, statement-making purple skirt.

Channel your elegant side and keep to the shade with this lovely lilac sun hat.

DEER

Put a spring in your step when you wear these fun flowery ankle bracelets.

You'll be as pretty as a bouquet in this refreshing floral necklace!

You're bound to be the most stylish deer at the beach in this colorful hat.

I'M READY TO "HOOT" IT TO THE BEACH!

FUN FACT

SWIM FINS, ALSO KNOWN AS FLIPPERS, ARE A TYPE OF WATER SHOE THAT LETS HUMANS SWIM MORE QUICKLY. FIRST INTRODUCED IN THE 1900S, THEY WERE INSPIRED BY MARINE MAMMALS' FLIPPERS!

SEAL

Gear up and hit the beach in some fashionable red flip-flops.

This tropical flower headpiece will help you soak up the sun!

Want to have tons of fun under the sun? This bright balloon is just the thing!

Showcase the spirit of summer with this trend-setting island necklace.

Keep cool as you hide out from the sun in these oversize sunglasses.

Water Wear

You've probably noticed that there's a reason you wear a special outfit for swimming—it repels water and dries out quickly. The same is true for animals that live in and around the water, although they don't use a swimsuit to stay dry. Instead, they rely on their fur to repel water and keep them warm.

Seals, otters, and many other marine mammals are able to trap a layer of air in between their fur and their skin, which lets them keep water out and keep heat in. Some animals, such as otters, also secrete an oily substance that helps further repel water.

DOUBLE UP

THE CLAW

OVERFLOW

PET WASH

TIERNEY'S TOUCH POOL

GREAT GAMES
IN CRYSTAL SANDS

BAHARI BAY

EVERYTHING IS PEACEFUL

DOWN IN THE BAY! BOB IN THE GENTLE WAVES AS THE RELAXING MUSIC WASHES OVER YOU.

TO GET TO BAHARI BAY, TAKE A WALK TO THE DOCK IN Crystal Sands and climb down the ladder. You'll find yourself in the beautiful waters of the bay. Swim with fierce barracudas and jellyfish, watch the kelp drift in the waves, and see if you can spot an elephant seal! Giant clams and sea cucumbers are abundant here. If you want to take a break from watching all the underwater life, head into Bahari Bargains. You'll find some great outfits for your ocean animals.

Paradise Bay: A lone sail skims the crystal clear bay water near Nelson, New Zealand.

BAHARI BARGAINS

Travel the seas in style with a little help from Bahari Bargains! This shop offers the latest in underwater fashions. Try on some seaweed hair, slip on some rainbow scales, or strap on some pufferfish spikes or a scuba helmet. To start shopping, swim through the double doors. You'll also find a recycling machine here where you can recycle unwanted items for Gems.

Down by the bay, where the dolphins and bears play! Bays are bodies of water that are partly enclosed by land with an outlet to the ocean. While people are fishing, crabbing, kayaking, and canoeing in bays, animals and plants are living in the waters and along the shore. The wildlife varies depending on where in the world the bay is located. Birds, fish, and insects can be found in all bay areas, while dolphins and manatees can be found splashing in some, and bears and bobcats can be seen on the shores of others!

Living on the Bay: A woman sells fruit on a boat in Vietnam's Ha Long Bay.

ALPHA TIP

Sir Gilbert

Are you a champion? If you win a game with four or more players, a special icon will appear above you to help you showcase your victory.

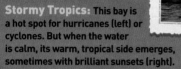

Stormy Tropics: This bay is a hot spot for hurricanes (left) or cyclones. But when the water is calm, its warm, tropical side emerges, sometimes with brilliant sunsets (right).

Bay of Bengal

One of the Seven Seas

TODAY, IF SOMEONE HAS SAILED the seven seas, it means they've traveled all the seas and oceans of the world! But to the ancient Arabs, the Seven Seas were the seven bodies of waters they sailed as part of their vital trading routes, and the Bay of Bengal was one of them.

The Bay of Bengal is the largest bay in the world and can be found in the northeastern Indian Ocean, bordered by India, Sri Lanka, Bangladesh, Myanmar, and the islands of Andaman and Nicobar. It's still part of an important trade route, and cargo from Sri Lanka, Bangladesh, and India pass through here.

Stormy weather is a part of the Bay of Bengal's climate. Monsoons are seasonal shifts in the wind's direction. These changes can bring heavy rains, thunderstorms, hail, and even tornadoes.

A cyclone is what a hurricane is called when it takes place in the Indian Ocean. These intense tropical storms happen in the Bay of Bengal during the spring and fall and bring fierce winds and flooding rains to the region.

Dreaded tsunamis also happen in this stormy bay. A tsunami is when massive waves crash from the sea onto land. These deadly waves are caused when an earthquake occurs under the sea.

Luckily, Bahari Bay is free of monsoons, cyclones, tsunamis, and other storms—a place where Jammers can play in gentle waves!

FUN FACT

BREEDING GROUNDS FOR THE ENDANGERED OLIVE RIDLEY SEA TURTLE ARE FOUND IN THE BAY OF BENGAL!

DOWN BY THE GULF!

DOWN BY THE BAY—OR DOWN BY THE GULF? LIKE A BAY, A GULF IS also partly surrounded by land. Usually gulfs are larger than bays, but not always. The Bay of Bengal occupies an area of 839,000 square miles (2,173,000 sq km), while the Gulf of Mexico is only 600,000 square miles (1,550,000 sq km).

There's no one clear defining factor to tell the two apart, but here's one tidbit of information you can tuck away for a trivia game: Both gulfs and bays have outlets to the ocean, but the outlets in gulfs are normally narrower than the wider bay ones. Whatever you call them, they're fun places to visit!

San Francisco's
Golden Gate Bridge

Bay-loving
harbor seals
bask in the sun.

San
Francisco Bay

The Golden
Gateway

MORE THAN 7 MILLION PEOPLE live in the cities and towns around the San Francisco Bay in California, U.S.A. The San Francisco Bay connects to the Pacific Ocean through the Golden Gate strait. You may have heard of the famous bridge that spans this strait, the Golden Gate Bridge! The bay itself is 60 miles (97 km) long and up to 12 miles (19 km) wide and contains beautiful harbors, many islands, and a multitude of wildlife species, including endangered ones.

Watch 18 species of whales in the bay and estuary, including blue whales and gray whales. Dolphins and porpoises play and hunt in the bay. Sharks, like the colorful leopard shark, live here, too.

The San Francisco Bay is also used as a nursery for all types of animals. For the broadnose sevengill sharks, it's one of two places they come to have their pups. Hundreds of species of birds nest here, including the endangered California clapper rail. Harbor seals come ashore to birth and raise their pups.

Common mammals like squirrels, rabbits, raccoons, and foxes live here, but mountain lions, bobcats, badgers, and elk also roam the bay area. Marine mammals like sea otters and elephant seals splash in the bay waters. Frogs, salamanders, newts, turtles, snakes, spiders, and butterflies are also plentiful!

Being so close to an urban landscape has drawbacks, the biggest being pollution. There are a number of wildlife organizations working to protect this amazing habitat that's so full of life.

FUN FACT

THE SAN FRANCISCO BAY'S ALCATRAZ ISLAND, HOME OF THE FORMER MAXIMUM SECURITY PRISON, WAS ALSO THE LOCATION OF THE FIRST LIGHTHOUSE ON THE WEST COAST OF THE UNITED STATES.

SO YOU WANT TO BE A

GET READY TO CHOMP DOWN ON SOME FUN!

IF CROCODILES LOOK LIKE LARGE PREHISTORIC reptiles, that's because they are! Crocodiles have roamed the Earth for 200 million years. These tough predators managed to survive when dinosaurs went extinct. Scientists believe these sturdy creatures have made it for so long because they are quick learners who can adapt to changes in their environment.

Crocodiles are reptiles that belong to the same order as alligators and caimans. There are 11 species within the genus *Crocodylus*.

These amphibious lizards are the largest and heaviest reptiles on the planet! Nocturnal hunters who spend most of their time in the water, they'll come to shore from time to time to bask in the sun to help regulate their body temperature.

STATS

SALTWATER CROCODILE

▸ **TYPE:** Reptile
▸ **DIET:** Water buffalo, monkeys, wild boar, and even sharks
▸ **LIFE SPAN:** 70 years
▸ **SIZE:** 17 feet (5 m)
▸ **WEIGHT:** 1,000 pounds (450 kg)
▸ **WHERE THEY LIVE:** Asia and Northern Australia

Croc Names: Saltwater crocs, the largest living crocs, are also called estuarine crocodiles.

crocodile?

CROC ADVENTURE

I know what it's like to want to be a crocodile. In fact, I practically was one myself!

I went to East Africa to field-test my protective croc suit. This specially designed equipment looks just like a crocodile with room for me to hide inside. The goal was to get close enough to a wild croc to attach a data device to it.

Once inside the suit, I crawled up to a group of wild crocs. When I got closer, one started hissing! Would my suit protect me?

It did! I got the device on the croc's back. I proved that I can use my disguise to study wild crocodiles close up without any harm to me or them. The data logger will provide us explorers with valuable data about these animals.

To see this exciting moment, stop by my lab and watch the video!

Are You a Crocodile?

IF THIS IS THE ANIMAL FOR YOU, YOU'RE PROBABLY THE KIND OF JAMMER WHO IS A TOUGH, QUICK-THINKER WHO KNOWS HOW TO GET BY IN ANY SITUATION.

149

Undersea Search!

CAN YOU FIND these OBJECTS IN THIS UNDERWATER SCENE? LOOK CAREFULLY!

Bonus! For more fun, count all the seahorses. Then find all the yellow fish. How many are there?

GREAT GAMES
IN BAHARI BAY

CRYSTAL REEF

AN UNDERWATER RAINBOW
OF VIVID COLOR GREETS YOU AS YOU SPLASH INTO CRYSTAL REEF!

THIS VIBRANT PLACE IS FILLED WITH PLANT AND ANIMAL life. Dive into the warm, crystal clear waters and get ready to explore! As you swim through the colorful coral and tube sponges, keep your eyes peeled for stingrays and even humpback whales!

While you're there, don't forget to visit Flippers 'N Fins to find the perfect aquatic pet.

153

Swimming With Coral: Divers take in the undersea sights off the Andaman Islands in the Indian Ocean.

Toxic Tail: Stingrays have poisonous barbs on their tails that are only used in self-defense.

Seahorses, turtles, jellies, and anglerfish are waiting to tag along on all of your ocean adventures and make loyal companions. To visit Crystal Reef, you'll need an ocean animal.

Like rain forests, coral reefs are home to a large variety of algal and animal life—25 percent of all recognizable, or macro, marine life lives in and around these beautiful environments! Found in clear, tropical oceans, reefs are living structures that are always changing.

Coral reefs are formed when baby coral, or larvae, swim through the water and attach themselves to a rock or another hard surface. The coral will remain there for the rest of its life without moving while it grows a hard skeleton. After the adult coral dies, the skeleton stays in place, creating the foundation for a coral reef!

DESTINATION A.J.

FLIPPERS 'N FINS

Tucked inside Crystal Reef is the pet shop Flippers 'N Fins. Swim to the door with the seahorse on it to start shopping for an ocean pet! You'll find the fierce anglerfish among other sea creatures here. A visit to the Pet Stop can change your fierce pet to cute, or a cuddly pet to tough. Play around with the different options to see what's offered for each pet. If you create an outfit you love, you can buy it for your pet.

Cool Coral Critters:
The Great Barrier Reef (right) is home to millions of creatures, like these yellow sponges (below), which may look like plants but are actually animals!

Great Barrier Reef
Wonder of the World

THE REAL-LIFE INSPIRATION FOR Crystal Reef and one of the seven wonders of the natural world, the magnificent Great Barrier Reef is larger than the Great Wall of China and is the only living thing on Earth visible from space!

The Great Barrier Reef is not one single reef but a sprawling group of about 3,000 individual reef systems. This biological treasure can be found off the east coast of Queensland, Australia, in the Coral Sea. As countless coral animals died, they left behind their skeletons bound together with algae, which formed the foundation of the reef. As reefs grow only about half an inch (1.3 cm) a year, the more than 1,400-mile (2,253-km)-long Great Barrier Reef took millions of years to form!

Teeming with marine life, the reef is home to over 1,500 species of tropical fish, hundreds of types of birds, and animals like prawns, dolphins, rays, sea turtles, clams, sharks, and crabs. The amazing coral gardens boast more than 400 different kinds of hard corals, the world's largest collection!

This wonder that took millions of years to make is shrinking in only decades! According to a 2012 study, the Great Barrier Reef has lost half of its coral over 27 years. Climate change, coastal storms, and crown-of-thorns starfish that feed on coral are to blame. The good news is if damaged reefs are protected from further harm, they can recover.

ALPHA TIP

COSMO

If you want to keep your cool when changing your animal's colors, click just to the right of the bottom purple swatch on the Change Your Looks screen to reveal the secret ice color.

HELPING REEFS

REEFS PROTECT MILLIONS OF PEOPLE AND ANIMALS.

CORAL REEFS AREN'T ONLY things of beauty. In addition to being home to countless marine life, reefs protect the shoreline and act as a buffer against waves, storms, and floods. Millions of people all over the world depend on these reefs not only for protection, but also for the jobs and food they provide. And like the rain forests they are compared to, coral reefs are home to plants that are being used in new medicines.

Valuable coral reefs all over the world are threatened by many factors. Everyone can do their share to protect these amazing underwater gardens by respecting all guidelines when visiting them. Even if you live thousands of miles away from a reef, you can help out by conserving water, recycling, and not polluting. Learn about reefs, like you're doing right now, and spread the news to your family and friends.

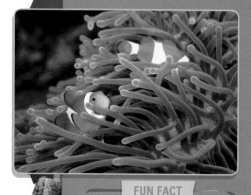

FUN FACT

CLOWNFISH MAKE THEIR HOME IN AN ANEMONE'S TENTACLES BUT DON'T GET STUNG BY THEM.

Crazy Coral Animals!

Coral reefs are home to some of the most beautiful and bizarre animals in the ocean!

Pygmy Seahorse

The adorable, tiny pygmy seahorse blends so well into its coral habitat that it's hard for predators to spot.

Moray Eel

The fierce moray eel is often confused with a sea snake. In place of fangs it has supersharp teeth!

Parrotfish

Yuck—a snot blanket! The parrotfish wraps itself up in a cocoon of its own mucus while sleeping.

Sea Snakes

Sea snakes have a poisonous bite and are fast swimmers. These aquatic snakes have to come up for air once every 20 or 30 minutes.

Nudibranch

These pretty mollusks don't have shells, but they make up for it by being some of the most colorful animals on Earth!

Coral Goby

These colorful fish are the defenders of a coral reef. They dine on invading seaweeds that threaten the reef's ecosystem.

SO YOU WANT TO BE A

Get ready to Have a "shell" time!

ABOUT 110 MILLION YEARS ago the first sea turtles navigated the Earth's oceans and seas. Today, seven species of sea turtles roam our waters. At up to 2,000 pounds (907 kg) and with a flipper span of 9 feet (2.7 m), the leatherback turtle is the largest, but it's tiny compared to its ancestor, the massive turtle, Archelon. It grew to be 15 feet (4.6 m) long and weighed as much as 4,000 pounds (1,814 kg), but it went extinct around the time of the dinosaurs.

Yet its descendants live on! Sea turtles are designed for maneuvering underwater, thanks to their streamlined shells, flippers that act as propellers, and webbed hind feet that work like rudders.

Are You a Sea Turtle?

KNOWN FOR THEIR GRACEFUL SWIMMING AND DETERMINATION WHEN IT COMES TO NESTING, TURTLES ARE THE PERFECT ANIMAL FOR JAMMERS WHO ARE POISED AND STRONG-MINDED!

Sea TurTle?

AMAZING SEA TURTLE NESTS

Every two to four years female green sea turtles will travel thousands of miles back to the beach where they were born to lay the eggs for the next generation of reptiles.

The largest green sea turtle nesting areas in the Western Hemisphere are in Costa Rica. The female turtles will dig as many as nine nests in one nesting season and will lay between 75 to 200 eggs per nest before covering them with sand and heading back to sea.

After about two months, the eggs will hatch tiny babies. As they rush to get to the sea, the hatchlings face a terrifying gauntlet of seabird predators that are waiting to make a meal out of them.

There are many challenges facing these turtles. Being hunted for their eggs and meat, accidental capture in fishing nets, and disease are some of their biggest threats. To help protect the turtles, people near nesting areas are asked to not disturb nesting sites.

Looking Out: Like other sea turtles, the green sea turtle can't pull its head into its shell.

STATS

GREEN SEA TURTLE

- **TYPE:** Reptile
- **DIET:** Sea grasses and algae
- **LIFE SPAN:** Over 80 years
- **SIZE:** Up to 5 ft (1.5 m)
- **WEIGHT:** Up to 700 pounds (317.5 kg)
- **STATUS:** Endangered
- **WHERE THEY LIVE:** Europe, North America, coastal waters from Alaska, U.S.A., to Chile

THREATS
to REEFS

CORALS FIGHT AGAINST SEA STAR BLOOMS.

WHILE THE HEALTH OF REEFS ALL OVER the world is threatened by both climate change and pollution, there's also an innocent-looking creature to blame. The crown-of-thorns starfish may be beautiful, but as one of the few animals that feed on living coral tissue it's a huge threat to reefs. These sea stars, which can have as many as 21 arms, are a natural part of the coral reef ecosystem in small numbers. But when conditions in the water cause the sea star population to explode, they eat corals faster than the corals can grow.

Spreading Fast: Female crown-of-thorns starfish, like this one in the Red Sea, can produce tens of millions of eggs a year.

When sea stars do bloom to excessively high numbers, it's often because of humans. Pollution from farms can flood coastal ocean waters with nutrients that baby sea stars feast on, increasing their population unnaturally. And it's not easy to fix. When an overabundance of crown-of-thorns starfish threatened the Great Barrier Reef in 2003, the Australian government spent millions to try to stop the destructive animals. But the irreplaceable Great Barrier Reef is worth every penny!

Getting Fishy: The Coral Triangle is home to millions of fish like these sweetlips fish (below) and the epaulette shark (right), which uses its fins like legs to walk along the seafloor.

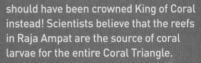

The Coral Triangle

Coral King

ONE REMOTE PART OF THE western Pacific Ocean holds the majority of the world's reef-building corals, almost 600 different species of them. This awesome coral treasure chest was given the name the Coral Triangle, and it boasts ten times the number of coral species found in the entire Caribbean Sea!

The stunning coral reefs that make up the triangle spread across the waters of Indonesia, Malaysia, the Philippines, Papua New Guinea, Timor-Leste, and the Solomon Islands. Approximately 80 percent of the world's coral species, more than 2,000 species of reef fish, and 6 of the world's 7 marine turtle species can be found in these remarkable underwater gardens.

The Raja Ampat Islands of Indonesia are found in the heart of the Coral Triangle. Raja Ampat means "four kings" but this archipelago, or group of islands,

should have been crowned King of Coral instead! Scientists believe that the reefs in Raja Ampat are the source of coral larvae for the entire Coral Triangle.

The Coral Triangle not only shelters countless fish, sea turtles, barracudas, seahorses, manta rays, and the rare "walking sharks" that use their fins like legs along coral reefs, but is also home to 120 million people. They rely on this marine metropolis for food, protection from storms, and to support themselves economically.

Cool Coral: These mushroom leather and lobed leather corals occupy a pristine reef in Indonesia.

A green sea turtle and various fish swim on the Great Barrier Reef in the South Pacific Ocean, Australia.

Reef Double Take

See if you can spot the 10 differences between these two pictures.

FUN FACT

GREEN SEA TURTLES ARE NAMED FOR THE GREENISH COLOR OF THEIR SKIN.

EAT LEAP UP

LOOK FOR this Great Game IN CRYSTAL REEF

Find the answers on page 232.

KANI COVE

SPLASH INTO KANI COVE TO EXPLORE THE RUINS OF A SHIP LOST BENEATH THE WAVES.

WARNING: THAR BE PIRATE TREASURE HERE! AS YOU explore, make sure to swim into the sunken ship's hull. Riches can be found for the taking in the Sunken Treasures shop. Pick up some plunder for your ocean den here!

Pirates aren't the only thing you need to keep a lookout for in Kani Cove. While you may spot a gentle manatee, a colorful parrotfish, or a tiny shrimp, hammerhead sharks also roam the waters here.

Sea Cow: Manatees may seem sluggish, but they can swim up to 15 miles an hour (25 kph) in short bursts.

HUNTING FOR TREASURE

Many treasure hunters hope to make a big profit by discovering priceless artifacts. About three million shipwrecks are thought to lie on the ocean floor. Searching for these has become big business, as companies are popping up to try to cash in on the ocean's treasures.

Hunting for shipwrecks is not easy. It's also very expensive. Some deep-sea explorations can cost up to $30 million! Yet it can pay off. But digging carelessly can destroy underwater archaeological sites. That's why the United Nations Educational, Scientific, and Cultural Organization (UNESCO) is encouraging governments, educators, and private businesses to work together to preserve the underwater cultural heritage of the world.

If you see any of these creatures, be sure to add them to your Journey Book!

There's a lot of exploring to do underwater! People who study and excavate these underwater shipwrecks are called maritime or nautical archaeologists. Maritime archaeologists also study ancient voyages, seafaring, and ships. Humans have been voyaging on the open seas for thousands of years. Lots of valuable evidence of sea travel can be found in our massive oceans, but as much as 95 percent of the world's ocean and 99 percent of the ocean floor are unexplored. Just imagine the wonders waiting to be discovered beneath the sea!

Pinning Prey: Hammerheads use their unusually shaped head to pin their favorite food, stingrays, to the seafloor.

Famous Bow: The *Titanic*'s bow is now covered in rust.

Stately Room: A light shows the interior of a first-class cabin.

The Titanic
The "Unsinkable" Ship

THE LARGEST MARITIME DISASTER in peacetime history occurred on April 15, 1912, when the luxury ocean liner R.M.S. *Titanic* sank into the icy depths of the North Atlantic Ocean. On her first voyage, the British ship hit an enormous iceberg. The *Titanic*, touted as "unsinkable," disappeared beneath the waves in less than three hours, costing the lives of 1,500 men, women, and children.

The ship's exact whereabouts remained a mystery until 1985, when oceanographer Robert Ballard discovered it about 560 miles (900 km) off the south of Newfoundland, Canada, using a submersible robot named Argo. Private salvage companies immediately went to work to gather artifacts from the sunken ship, until laws were passed making it illegal to remove anything from the wreckage without official approval. Expensive clothing, jewelry, perfumes, shoes, reading glasses, and fixtures from the ship itself, such as lights, signs, windows, and even toilets, are among the items recovered.

Underwater cinematographers traveled 13,000 feet (3,962 m) to the ocean floor to capture haunting video of the *Titanic* in its watery grave. The tragic sinking of this great ship has inspired movies, plays, and a fascination that still exists 100 years later.

Today, the *Titanic* is fighting another losing battle: time. The huge ship is an ocean-floor buffet for marine organisms. The wood of the ship has been eaten by mollusks while microscopic bacteria and fungi munch away on the metal hull. As they eat, they create rust icicles, which now cover the *Titanic*'s bow. But oceanographers are working on ideas on how to preserve this piece of history.

Remembering the Titanic: The ocean liner was luxurious, as shown in this photograph of the grand staircase (left). No expense was spared, like this spoon (below) that elaborately spells out R.M.S. *Titanic* on the handle.

FINDING SHIPWRECKS

UNDISCOVERED SHIPWRECKS and lost treasure have an air of excitement and romance about them. They allow a person's imagination to wander and have been the subject of countless tales. But there's a downside to these underwater relics.

Military ships, cargo vessels, pirate ships, and tankers transporting everything from oil to chemicals have sunk to the bottom of the ocean. Many of them could potentially be leaking pollutants into the sea.

Thirty-six sunken ships off the coast of the United States were identified by the National Oceanic and Atmospheric Administration (NOAA) as posing a threat of oil pollution. Knowing where these ships are can help cleanup efforts if a spill is reported in the area.

Amazing Shipwreck Treasures

Here are just some of the treasures that have been discovered beneath the ocean waves!

Show off a little shipwreck bling! This 10-carat emerald and gold ring, found in a shipwreck in the Florida Keys, U.S.A., is valued at half a million dollars.

The mysterious Antikythera mechanism, recovered from a shipwreck off of Greece, is 2,000 years old and contains 30 different types of interlocking gears. Today archaeologists believe it's an astronomical calendar.

An incredible $36 million worth of silver was found off the coast of Ireland in the S.S. *Gairsoppa*. This British cargo ship was torpedoed by a Nazi U-boat during World War II.

Pirate Leader: An illustration shows Captain Bartholomew Roberts with his two ships the *Royal Fortune* and the *Ranger*.

PIRATES HAVE BEEN around for thousands of years. Ever since humans figured out how to transport valuables by water they've been plagued by pirates!

The way to the most infamous age in piracy was paved by Queen Elizabeth I of England. Dubbed the "Pirate Queen" by her enemies, she asked her best sailors to become privateers and loaned them ships and supplies to attack boats from other countries, especially Spain. The queen split the spoils with her pirates, such as famous privateers Sir Walter Raleigh and Sir Francis Drake. Everyone was happy—except for the Spaniards,

Pirates! Ahoy, Matey!

Royal Jaws: Elizabeth I had black teeth.

that is. They were definitely not pleased.

But why share the loot when you can keep it all for yourself? During the first quarter of the 1700s, dubbed the "golden age of piracy," thousands made a living by becoming pirates. This is when famous pirates like Blackbeard, Major Stede Bonnet, Captain "Calico Jack" Rackham, and Bartholomew "Black Bart" Roberts ruled the seas!

Cheers! Salvagers found 168 unbroken bottles of champagne in a wreck in the Baltic Sea from the 1820s. One bottle alone sold for $37,400—and the champagne's still drinkable!

The sea was paved with gold! A 1622 wreck of a Spanish ship, the *Atocha*, dropped over 185,000 silver and 120 gold coins along the ocean floor.

DESTINATION A.J.

SUNKEN TREASURES

If you've been searching the ocean depths for fantastic treasures, your search is over! Kani Cove's Sunken Treasures, located in the hull of a sunken ship, gives you an opportunity to decorate your ocean den in the colors of the sea and with amazing ocean life!

SO YOU WANT TO BE A SHARK?

WHY MESS WITH PERFECTION? SHARKS HAVE EXISTED on Earth for 400 million years and have changed little in the last 200 million. Their ancient design allows for speed and maneuverability coupled with a super sense of smell. The hungrier the shark is, the better it can smell you, my dear!

But no need to skip that ocean vacation with your family. Very few species of sharks attack humans. In 2012, only 80 shark attacks were reported worldwide. The odds of being bitten by a shark are 1 in 11.5 million!

Earth's oceans are home to approximately 500 species of sharks. These range from the dwarf lantern shark, which is only 8 inches (20 cm) long, to the enormous, 40-foot (12-m)-long whale shark, the largest fish in the sea!

TAKE A BITE OUT OF JAMAA!

Are You a Shark?

IF YOU LIKE TO SNIFF YOUR FOOD BEFORE YOU EAT IT AND HAVE A KILLER SMILE, THE SHARK IS THE PERFECT JAMAA ANIMAL FOR YOU!

POWER SNIFFERS

Sharks have some of the most sophisticated snouts in the area. Great whites can smell blood from miles away. The scent organs in their snouts have amazing sniffing abilities. In fact, the part of the shark's brain dedicated to smell, or olfaction, is unusually large compared with other animals.

Blood isn't the only thing these sharks can detect. Thanks to amazing organs called ampullae of Lorenzini, sharks can sense when another animal's muscles are contracting!

Shark Senses: Ampullae of Lorenzini look like small black dots on a shark's snout.

The ampullae, located in the snout, help the shark sense electromagnetic fields.

STATS

GREAT WHITE SHARK

▸ **TYPE:** Fish
▸ **DIET:** Sea lions, seals, small-toothed whales, sea turtles, and carrion (dead and decaying animals)
▸ **LIFE SPAN:** 30 years
▸ **SIZE:** 15 feet (4.6 m) to more than 20 feet (6 m)
▸ **WEIGHT:** 5,000 pounds (2,268 kg) or more
▸ **STATUS:** Endangered
▸ **WHERE THEY LIVE:** Nearly all of the world's oceans and seas, mostly temperate coastal areas

Fishy Fast: Great white sharks poke their heads out of the water to pick up airborne scents.

FUN FACT

THE GREAT WHITE SHARK HAS THE LARGEST TEETH OF ANY LIVING SHARK— TWO INCHES (5 CM) LONG!

STUDYING SHIPWRECKS

PRESERVED WRECKS ARE A LOOK BACK IN TIME.

A SINKING SHIP WAS AN unlucky thing for anyone who happened to be on board! But for historians, the remains of these underwater disasters are often a fortunate gift. Well-preserved shipwrecks serve as time capsules, giving a rare glimpse into the past. When conditions are right, such as cold water and little marine life, some of these ships and their cargo can remain perfectly preserved.

In 2012, an amazingly well-preserved shipwreck was found in the Gulf of Mexico. Muskets and cannons were discovered with the wreck, leading researchers to speculate that the ship possibly belonged to pirates!

PIRATES MADE THEIR PRISONERS (OR EACH OTHER) WALK THE PLANK.

Forcing someone to walk the plank and plunge into the ocean was an uncommon practice. Pirates will forever be associated with it thanks to two fictional tales: *Treasure Island* by Robert Louis Stevenson and *Peter Pan* by J.M. Barrie. The truth is that pirate punishments were a lot more gruesome. Pirate justice included whipping, torture, marooning, and keelhauling, a practice in which a pirate bound to a rope was dragged down one side of the ship, underneath it, and then up the other side.

PIRATES WERE ONLY MEN.

Not true! Ferocious female pirates Anne Bonny and Mary Read were respected by their crews for both their toughness and their fighting skills.

PIRATES BURIED THEIR TREASURE.

Once a ship was plundered or a town looted, pirates wanted their share pronto! Spoils were quickly divided and rarely hidden or buried. Again, this piece of popular pirate lore is thanks to the novel *Treasure Island*.

PIRATES DON'T EXIST ANYMORE.

As long as people continue to travel by water, there will be pirates. In 2012, 297 ships were attacked by pirates. Most of these attacks took place off the coasts of East and West Africa.

Pirate Treasure Search

CAN YOU FIND ALL THE PIRATE BOOTY IN THIS SCENE? LOOK CAREFULLY!

6 treasure chests
3 cannons
1 stack of gold bars
1 spyglass
2 swords

3 eye patches
1 antique
treasure map
2 hooks
4 bombs

Bonus! Count your loot: How many gold coins can you find?

Find the answers on page 233.

DEEP BLUE

AS YOU SWIM DEEPER, BE PREPARED TO SEE THE MOST UNUSUAL CREATURES IN THE WORLD!

P

LUNGING INTO THE DEEPEST WATERS OF JAMAA'S oceans, you'll be greeted by eerie squid and translucent jellies! The lack of sunlight at the bottom of ocean trenches like Deep Blue means the animals live in an almost pitch-black environment, causing many of them to lack color and to develop other odd physical characteristics. Instead of making you feel as if you are miles underneath the water, these bizarre organisms can make you believe you're on another planet!

Prepare to Dive: This submersible, called DeepSee, is used by filmmakers and is capable of carrying three people to depths of 1,500 feet (475 m).

As you dive even farther into these quiet, gloomy waters you may even stumble across some treasure!

Most ocean trenches are located in the largest ecosystem on Earth, the deep sea. Trenches are long, deep depressions carved into the ocean floor. The movement of tectonic plates is what forms these marine chasms. The deepest parts of the oceans, and in fact, of the entire Earth, are found in ocean trenches. They range from 24,000 feet (7.3 km) to 36,000 feet (11 km) deep.

IN THE FIELD WITH TIERNEY THYS

DIVING DEEP

Exploring the ocean is tricky. One of the most obvious reasons is that people cannot breathe underwater! The first snorkel was a hollow reed early swimmers used to breathe air. Diving suits and air pumps paved the way for modern scuba-diving gear. That solved one problem. But the deeper divers wanted to go, the more intense the water pressure.

High water pressure during deep-water dives can put stress on the body that can injure the heart and lungs, but there are a number of ways divers can adjust to these pressure changes safely. No ordinary gear can be used to explore the extreme depths of the ocean. Submarines and robots let us explore the very bottom.

Studies of the deep ocean are important because this environment can help us research life's origins as well as earthquakes that cause deadly tsunamis.

Alien Life: This small plankton (left) and long red-lined sea cucumber can be found in the deep ocean.

YOU'LL HAVE to dive deep, deep underneath the waves to explore one of the most remote and strangest places on Earth: the Mariana Trench!

Located in the western Pacific Ocean, this crescent-shaped trench has a depth of 36,201 feet (11,034 m)—over 6 miles (9.7 km) deep! It's also five times the length of the Grand Canyon and spans 43 miles (69 km) wide. If Mount Everest, the tallest mountain in the world, were dropped into the Mariana Trench, its peak would still be more than a mile (1.6 km) underwater. Thousands of climbers have scaled Mount Everest, yet only three people have been able to descend into the deepest part of the Mariana Trench.

The Mariana Trench was discovered by the H.M.S. *Challenger* in 1875 during the first global oceanographic cruise. The depths of the trench were plumbed again by the *Challenger II* in 1951. The deepest part of the trench, Challenger Deep, was named after these pioneering vessels. Descents into the trench took place in 1960 and 2012.

Aquatic life-forms inhabit the trench at different depths, including shrimp-like amphipods, translucent holothurians or sea cucumbers, anglerfish, and eels. Life at the bottom of Challenger Deep used to be thought of as scarce. That's because the water pressure here is like having 50 jumbo jets piled on top of you! Yet some of the world's earliest forms of life, single-celled organisms called foraminifera, are thriving in great numbers in the seafloor here.

Mariana Trench

Deepest Place on Earth

	SEA LEVEL
Deepest scuba dive	
Deepest recorded sperm whale dive	10,000 ft. 3,048 m
H.M.S. *Titanic* wreckage	
	15,000 ft. 4,572 m
	20,000 ft. 6,096 m
	25,000 ft. 7,620 m
Height of Mount Everest	30,000 ft. 9,144 m
Challenger Deep	35,000 ft. 10,668 m

SO YOU WANT TO BE AN

MONSTER OF THE DEEP, INTELLIGENT sea creature, or delicious delicacy? Found in oceans throughout the world, the octopus is known for its bulging eyes, rounded body, and of course its eight limbs! It also has an awesome swimming stunt. The octopus can swim backward by blasting water through a tube on its body called a siphon.

The octopus is a mollusk like clams, oysters, and snails. The smallest octopus, the *O. arborescens* species, is only about 2 inches (5 cm) long. On the other side of the spectrum is the giant Pacific octopus. The biggest one ever recorded was 30 feet (9.1 m) long and weighed over 600 pounds (272 kg)!

IN THE FIELD WITH TIERNEY THYS

EXPERT ESCAPE ARTISTS

Octopuses are stealthy marine animals that are very ninja-like in the way they evade predators and disappear into their surroundings.

To escape detection, the octopus can change its color to gray, brown, pink, blue, or green to blend in with its surroundings. Many times a hungry hunter will pass right by the octopus without even seeing it!

If a seal or shark does spot it, the octopus can shoot out an inky fluid and make a getaway. They can also tuck themselves into small places where predators can't reach them. And if

Atlantic white-spotted octopus

something does manage to chomp down on one of the octopus's eight arms, a new one will grow back. That's arm-azing!

OCTOPUS?

GET READY TO LEND A HAND TO ALL YOUR BUDDIES!

Supersmarts: Octopuses are smart and can open jars, mimic other octopuses, and even solve puzzles!

Are You an Octopus?

KNOWN FOR THEIR INTELLIGENCE AND STEALTH, THIS IS A GREAT ANIMAL FOR SMART JAMMERS WHO HAVE NINJA SKILLS!

STATS

GIANT PACIFIC OCTOPUS

▶ **TYPE:** Invertebrate
▶ **DIET:** Shrimp, clams, lobsters, fish, sharks, and seabirds
▶ **LIFE SPAN:** 3 to 5 years
▶ **SIZE:** 9.75 to 16 feet (3 to 5 m)
▶ **WEIGHT:** 22 to 110 pounds (10 to 50 kg)
▶ **WHERE THEY LIVE:** Temperate water of the Pacific, from southern California to Alaska, U.S.A., west to the Aleutian Islands and Japan

MONSTERS OF THE DEEP

TO SURVIVE IN THE DEEPEST place on Earth, deep-sea organisms have to adapt to total darkness, crushing pressures, and cold water temperatures.

Living in the dark means that many organisms that live in the deep sea lack color or are transparent. Some look like they could be aliens from another world!

Many of these animals feast on decaying microbes, algae, plants, and dead animals from the upper zones of the ocean that have sunk to the bottom. When the hagfish comes across a carcass, it burrows into it and then eats the decaying corpse from the inside out!

Another unique adaptation of ocean trench animals is deep-sea gigantism. Most famous is the elusive giant squid. The biggest one ever recorded was 43 feet (13 m) long and may have weighed nearly a ton (0.9 MT)!

Deep-Sea Creatures

Meet some of the deep-sea denizens that live in ocean trenches. Scientists believe that many more unusual animals are just waiting to be discovered in these vast unexplored areas of the world!

▲ Anglerfish

The appendage sticking over the anglerfish's mouth is a dorsal spine that the fish uses as a fishing pole! The tip of the spine is bioluminescent, or glowing, and acts as a lure to attract smaller fish.

Hatchetfish

Built-in night-lights! The organs that line the belly of this bizarre-looking fish glow as bright as daylight and are used to confuse predators.

Alien Deep: Below, crabs crawl over Riftia tubes growing on hydrothermal vents. At right, deep-sea vents spew minerals that form when the hot fluid mixes with seawater.

Hydrothermal Vents

Deep-Sea Smokers

THE GEYSERS OF THE OCEAN floor are hydrothermal vents. Hot water is pushed out through the vents as seawater circulates through volcanic rocks. As a result, these deep-sea smokers emit warm, mineral-rich water that contains iron, copper, zinc, and hydrogen sulfide.

This mineral concoction works as a substitute for sunlight to the organisms that live in the deep sea. They can't use photosynthesis, the process by which plants make energy from sunlight that most life on Earth depends on. Instead, the vents allow chemosynthesis to take place. It's a process that organisms use to make food without needing sunlight.

Chemosynthesis makes hydrothermal vents a popular place to live in the deep sea! Thriving chemical-based communities surround these vents, and it's the only system on Earth where life can flourish with zero sunlight. The life that is supported here includes tube worms, fish, crabs, octopuses, snails, and clams.

Scientists believe these amazing environments could be the birthplace where life on Earth began! The reaction between the salty ocean water and the chemicals produced from hydrothermal vents might have paved the way for the first biological molecules on the planet.

Viperfish

The viperfish's jagged, needle-like teeth are so big that these fish can't close their mouths. They use the glowing organs in their body to lure in prey.

Giant Squid

A giant squid's eyeballs are the same size as a beach ball! Those huge eyes help the creature see in the murky waters it lives in.

Gulper Eel

Gulper eels get their names from their enormous mouths, and some have mouths longer than their bodies. Their stomachs can expand, allowing these eels to eat food bigger than they are.

AMAZING AQUATIC ANIMALS

#1 About how many years ago did sea turtles first appear on the planet?

a. 10,000 years ago
b. 60 million years ago
c. 110 million years ago
d. 5,000 years ago

#2 Which of these animals sometimes hops on a floating piece of ice to get from place to place?

a. Dolphin
b. Polar bear
c. Crocodile
d. Harp seal

#3 The largest living crocodile is the:

a. Saltwater crocodile
b. Nile crocodile
c. American crocodile
d. African dwarf crocodile

#4 Orcas are members of the dolphin family.

True or False?

#5 Which of these sea creatures has existed on Earth the longest?

a. Sea otter
b. Crocodile
c. Dolphin
d. Sea turtle

#6 Which of the following animals' diet consists of living coral?

a. Coral goby
b. Green-banded snapping shrimp
c. Sea snake
d. Crown-of-thorns starfish

#7 This animal's enormous eyeball is the size of a beach ball:

a. Giant squid
b. Orca
c. Blue whale
d. Stingray

#8 Penguins are only found north of the Equator.

True or False?

#9 Orcas live in groups called:

a. Schools
b. Teams
c. Pods
d. Herds

#10 Dolphins are found not only in oceans but in some rivers, too.

True or False?

#11 The octopus cannot swim backward.

True or False?

#12 How big is the smallest shark in the world?

a. 8 inches (20 cm)
b. 40 feet (12 m)
c. 3.5 feet (1.1 m)
d. 16 inches (41 cm)

#13 Crocodiles lived on Earth when dinosaurs were alive.

True or False?

#14 This fish uses a modified fin spine as a fishing pole to lure in prey:

a. Clown anemonefish
b. Hatchetfish
c. Viperfish
d. Anglerfish

#15 How did the harp seal get its name?

a. They love music.
b. There's a harp-shaped mark on its back.
c. Harp was the last name of the person who discovered the species.
d. They make a noise that sounds like a harp being played.

PHANTOM'S TREASURE

LOOK FOR THIS GREAT GAME

IN DEEP BLUE

Find the answers on page 233.

MT. SHIVEER

GET READY TO CLIMB THE HIGHEST MOUNTAIN IN JAMAA!

HERE YOU CAN LET YOUR INNER EXPLORER PLAY WILD! Once you've made it to the top of Mt. Shiveer, get back to the bottom by whooshing down the ice slide. All that snow and ice is chilling, but there are plenty of places to warm up here. Take a dip in the natural hot springs, or head into the Hot Cocoa Hut to get toasty warm with a hot beverage or by shopping for some cozy winter clothes.

Snowcapped Peaks: The sun rises over Cerro Torre mountain in Argentina's Andes mountain range.

Mountain Animals: Yaks (above), wild boar (above right), and common tahr (right) live in the Himalaya.

Rocky cliffs, little vegetation, and extreme temperature changes make this environment a place where only the strong survive. No animals or vegetation can live at the very top of high mountains like Mount Everest. Yet in the lower levels of the Himalayan mountain range, and in the surrounding forests and valleys, you can find bears, leopards, wolves, wild boar, yaks, and hoofed animals like the muntjac, serow, and tahr.

To be a mountain, you've got to be tall! Mountains are pieces of land that rise significantly higher than the area around them. When a piece of protruding land rises over 2,000 feet (610 m) tall, it's usually considered a mountain.

Both people and animals make their homes in mountain ranges around the world. It's not an easy place to live, especially the higher you climb.

PECK

ALPHA TIP

When you visit Mt. Shiveer, you might find yourself on thin ice—literally! Many Jammers like to go and stand on the frozen pond with the caution sign. They'll even start jumping up and down on it! The ice will crack, but has never completely broken. Yet.

Top of the World: Sherpas play horseshoes underneath Tibetan prayer flags on Mount Everest (right). An aerial view of the mountain (below) shows its massive size.

Mount Everest
High Hopes

IMAGINE THE 103-FLOOR EMPIRE State Building stacked on top of itself 20 times! This fantastic height is the same as that of the world's highest summit, and real-life inspiration for Mt. Shiveer, Mount Everest. It towers in the Himalaya of southern Asia at 29,035 feet (8,850 m). Located on the border of Nepal and Tibet, this mystical mountain has been beckoning explorers to climb its lofty heights for decades.

Even before the rest of the world started beating a path to the base of Mount Everest, it was home to the Sherpas who live on the southern side of the mountain. They have adapted to the high altitude and cold of mountain life. They've helped lead almost every climbing expedition on Mount Everest.

Eventually, European mountaineers arrived on the scene. George Mallory discovered the northern approach to the mighty mountain in 1921. He's responsible for the famous line "Because it's there" when asked why he wanted to climb Mount Everest. He would never make it to the top. While trying to reach the summit in 1924, Mallory died.

He's not the only one to perish scaling the harshest, tallest mountain in the world. Climbing the mountain is dangerous due to harsh temperatures, avalanches, blizzards, and lack of oxygen.

The first people to successfully reach the summit were Edmund Hillary and Sherpa Tenzing Norgay on May 29, 1953. As long as Mount Everest continues rising high into the sky, there will be people who will want to scale this magnificent mountain. Why? Because it's there!

High Climbers: Sherpa Tenzing Norgay (left) and Edmund Hillary (right) reached Mount Everest's summit in 1953.

MOUNT EVEREST IS THE HEIGHT OF MORE THAN 20 EMPIRE STATE BUILDINGS!

SO YOU WANT to BE AN EAGLE?

STATS

BALD EAGLE

▸ **TYPE:** Bird
▸ **DIET:** Fish, small mammals
▸ **LIFE SPAN:** Up to 28 years
▸ **SIZE:** Up to 43 inches (109 cm); wingspan, up to 8 feet (2.4 m)
▸ **WEIGHT:** 6.5 to 14 pounds (3 to 6.5 kg)
▸ **WHERE THEY LIVE:** North America

IN THE FIELD WITH DR. BRADY BARR

PROTECTING BALD EAGLES

The bald eagle proves that when people protect endangered animals they can be saved! When these birds were first named the national bird of America, they numbered up to 100,000. Hunting and a pesticide called DDT dropped the number of bald eagles to only about 450 nesting pairs by the 1960s. But when the use of DDT was banned in 1972, the number of bald eagles began to rise again.

By 2007, more than 9,700 nesting pairs were counted in the wild and the bald eagle was removed from the endangered species list!

TaKE to the SKIES!

STRONG AND MAJESTIC, THE EAGLE has been a symbol of power for many years. The Greeks and Romans used this bird of strength on their coins and medals. The bald eagle has been the national symbol of the United States of America since 1782.

The term "eagle" is applied to a bird of prey that is more powerful than a buzzard or hawk and whose diet mainly consists of eating live animals, rather than scavenging on carrion, or an animal that is already dead.

Swooping quickly down from above, the eagle uses the element of surprise to catch its prey off-guard. Many eagles are also fantastic fishers and can spy a fish in the water up to a mile (1.6 km) away!

Bald eagles build their nests, or aeries, at the top of tall trees or cliffs with branches and twigs. These birds build big! One of the largest nests ever found was 9 feet (2.7 m) wide and 20 feet (6.1 m) deep and weighed more than 4,000 pounds (1,814 kg)!

Are You an Eagle?

POWERFUL AND FAST EAGLES ARE PERFECT ANIMALS FOR JAMMERS WHO ARE STRONG AND SPEEDY!

Growing Up Bald: It takes about five years for a young bald eagle to reach adulthood and have a completely white head and tail.

MOUNTAINS AND PEOPLE

LIVING HIGH UP TOGETHER!

King of the Mountain

To make it up high, you've got to be mighty! Animals need special skills to live in mountainous terrain. Check out how these animals survive.

Cool Kicks

Athletic sneakers have got nothing on the incredible footwear sported by hoofed animals that live in rocky regions! Mountain goats, llamas, and ibex have specially designed feet that help them move easily along rocky ground.

Fur and Furnaces

Many mountain animals, like the yak and alpaca, have thick fur coats to protect them against frigid temps. The rumen, a chamber of the yak's stomach, can heat up to 104°F (40°C), keeping the animal warm.

It's in Their Blood

Llamas have a unique way of dealing with the lack of oxygen. Their blood contains a very high concentration of red blood cells, which helps deliver more oxygen throughout their bodies!

Tough Teeth

The sparse vegetation in some areas of the mountain is tough and hard to eat. To chow down, many herbivores have big and sturdy chompers.

MOUNTAINS AREN'T EASY TO CLIMB OR live in but humans have been reaping the rewards of these hilly environments throughout time.

On fertile mountain slopes in Java, Guatemala, and Sicily, people grow tea and coffee in lower zones and graze cattle on the rich grass found higher up. Mountains provide fresh water, timber, and minerals, as well as beautiful and scenic vacation spots. But the risk of doing business in some mountain landscapes is avalanches and landslides!

Mountain ranges can also act like natural security walls. High mountains bordering Switzerland have protected it from attacks and involvement in several wars. In order to attack Rome, Hannibal, the military leader of Carthage, had to make a treacherous trek across the Alps in 218 B.C. with thousands of troops, horses, and about 40 elephants—no easy feat!

DESTINATION A.J.

THE HOT COCOA HUT

After taking an exhilarating zip down Mt. Shiveer's ice slide, cozy up with a warm drink inside the Hot Cocoa Hut. Inside the colorful tent you can choose a delicious warm beverage made with your choice of toppings. Curl up on one of the comfy blankets scattered around the room as you listen to the wind blow outside. Or do a little shopping here at the Shiveer Shoppe and pick out a winter outfit that will protect you from Mt. Shiveer's icy weather!

SO YOU WANT to be a SNOW LEOPARD?

SHOW OFF YOUR *PURR-FECTION!*

IN THE FIELD WITH DR. BRADY BARR

HELPING SNOW LEOPARDS

Snow leopards are endangered, but they have a lot of friends looking out for them! In Tibet, the snow leopards' territory is shared by many Buddhist monasteries. It turns out the monks who live there are great neighbors to these beautiful cats! They go out on patrols to protect the snow leopards from potential poachers. The monks are also educating other people in the area about why it's important not to harm these animals.

IT'S EASY TO SEE HOW THESE BIG CATS GOT THEIR nickname, "ghost cat." Unlike darker leopards, the snow leopard is a lighter gray color with less distinctive, almost blurry, spots, and a snow-white tummy. The effect is beautiful as well as helpful. Snow leopards live in the mountains of Central Asia and India, and its coat helps it blend into its snowy and rocky surroundings.

Snow leopards' coats are also thick and dense, creating a natural insulation against the cold temperatures. These cats have built-in snowshoes, thanks to their furry feet, which help give traction on slippery surfaces.

But snow leopards are endangered due to poaching and habitat decline. Scientists are working on learning more about this rare and elusive creature, to figure out the best ways to protect them.

STATS

SNOW LEOPARD

▸ TYPE: Mammal
▸ DIET: Blue sheep (bharal), ibex, marmots, hares, and game birds
▸ LIFE SPAN: 20 years (in captivity)
▸ SIZE: 4 to 5 feet (1.2 to 1.5 m); tail, 36 inches (91 cm)
▸ WEIGHT: 60 to 120 pounds (27 to 54 kg)
▸ STATUS: Endangered
▸ WHERE THEY LIVE: Asia

Cozy Tails: A snow leopard uses its tail like a blanket in really cold weather.

Are You a Snow Leopard?

IF THE SNOW LEOPARD IS THE ANIMAL FOR YOU, YOU'RE MOST LIKELY THE KIND OF JAMMER WHO ALWAYS WINS AT GAMES OF HIDE AND SEEK! LIKE THE ELUSIVE SNOW LEOPARD, YOU LIKE BEING ALONE.

MAKING A MOUNTAIN

SLOW-GROWING GIANTS!

THE POPULAR SAYING IS TRUE— mountains can be made out of molehills! Or rocks, dirt, twigs, or anything else on the ground when the Earth's plates collide!

Earth's outer layer is made up of plates called the lithosphere. When plates underneath landmasses move and collide, the crust of the earth crumbles and buckles to form mountain ranges. The mountains found on our planet are evidence of the plates moving long ago. The Himalaya began to be formed 45 million years ago during a collision of continental plates. To this day, the plates that slid underneath each other to form this mountain range are still slowly moving, growing the mountains by millimeters each year!

IN THE FIELD WITH DR. BRADY BARR

MOUNTAIN MONSTER

A powerful and giant creature, towering over 6 feet (2 m) tall and covered with brown, matted hair. Is the yeti, or the abominable snowman, fact or fiction?

No one has ever been able to prove the existence of this wild man of the mountain. Sightings of large footprints in the snow and of a beast walking on two legs have been reported for years in the Himalayan mountains.

Nonbelievers offer this explanation: bears. But a lack of evidence doesn't deter die-hard yeti fanatics. Even in modern times, new species are discovered in rain forests and the oceans all the time. The vast majority of the Himalaya are unexplored with no one living there. If such a creature as the yeti did exist, wouldn't this mountain range be the perfect place for it to hide? One can only imagine!

Arctic Headgear: Musk oxen (below) have horns, which males use to compete for mates; walruses (right) have ivory tusks, which males use to protect their females and to pull themselves out of the water!

EVER FEEL LIKE YOU'RE ON THE top of the world? People use that expression when they're feeling happy. But it would be more accurate to say when you're feeling cold!

That's because the northernmost part of the world, the North Pole, is surrounded by a vast and icy area known as the Arctic. Most of the Arctic is covered with ocean and floating sea ice. The majority of the land in the Arctic is in the Arctic Circle, which runs parallel to the Equator, and is found in Asia, Europe, and North America. The Arctic Circle encompasses 6 percent of the total surface area of the Earth. The land in the Arctic Circle is tundra, which is marked by cold temperatures; dry, powerful winds; and permanently frozen soil called permafrost.

Jamaa's Mt. Shiveer is based on the Arctic's chilly climes. Even though this inhospitable place contains less wildlife than other habitats of the world, life still exists here. Polar bears and arctic foxes hunt, caribou and musk ox graze on the sparse grasses, and small collared lemmings hibernate in the permafrost. In the Arctic Ocean, whales, polar bears, walruses, seals, and sharks roam the waters and coasts.

It's hard to imagine people living in this hostile land, but societies were built around the hunting and fishing that this region of the world offers. The Inuit people are just one of dozens of native peoples of the Arctic.

Today, weather and polar research stations are found in the Arctic where glaciologists study the ice and snow, biologists investigate climate change, oceanographers explore the mysteries of the ocean, and astronomers look to the skies!

WHO WORE it BEST?

IN JAMAA, WHO WEARS IT BEST? EVERYONE! With tons of fun clothing and accessories to choose from, you'll always be best dressed. Let's check out how these snow leopards and arctic wolves take hats to new heights. Which do you like the best?

Be the prettiest wolf at the Wolves'-Only Party with this cute pink wig.

The party never has to end with this fun and lively hat!

ARCTIC WOLF

When you wear this feathered mask, you'll feel like you can fly!

Be at the TOP of the best-dressed list when you sport this founder's hat.

As if wolves weren't tough enough already, just add horns for some extra danger in your look.

OBVIOUSLY I'VE GOT THIS IN THE BAG.

FUN FACT

FEATHERS ON HATS WERE A HUGE FASHION TREND IN THE 1900s. BUT THIS STYLE CAME WITH A BIG PRICE. THE HIGH DEMAND FOR FEATHERS THREATENED SOME BIRD SPECIES WITH EXTINCTION. TODAY LAWS RESTRICT THE USE OF ORNAMENTAL FEATHERS.

With this rare and lavish hat, you'll be sure to make a statement.

What happens when you cross a snow leopard with a rhino? This!

SNOW LEOPARD

Perfect for when you want to go undercover to spy on what the Phantoms are up to.

Watch out, if you wear this delicious-looking hat, someone might take a bite out of it!

Put this helmet on your head to show the warrior within.

Arctic Animals

Each season, designers put out their latest clothing collections. But humans aren't the only ones who change their look with the weather. Many arctic animals do, too.

Animals such as the arctic fox, snowshoe hare, and the ermine undergo a transformation every winter. During the spring, their fur is darker. But in the fall, their bodies start to make less of the pigment melanin, which is the substance inside hair or feathers that gives them color. By the time winter comes, these animals' coats are a dazzling white!

GEM BREAKER

COCOA MACHINE

GREAT GAMES
IN MT. SHIVEER

KiMBara
OUTBACK

A DrY, DUSTY WIND WHiPS AGAiNST your FACE as YOU STEP ONTO the SUN-BAKED GROUND OF the WiLD OUTBACK!

RUGGED ROCK FORMATIONS SURROUND YOU. A WATERFALL courses down a rocky cliff, and you stop to take a dip in the cool water. Feeling refreshed, you climb onto the bridge to soak in the sweeping panoramas of deserts and grasslands. A strange bird, unlike any you've ever seen, runs away as you approach. You have a feeling you're going to see a lot more exotic animals and plants as you explore Kimbara Outback!

DESTINATION A.J.

OUTBACK IMPORTS

You'll find the rugged Outback Imports carved into a rocky cliff on top of Kimbara Outback's waterfalls. Durable furniture and other items built to last in the harsh Outback environment are for sale here, so grab your mates and get shopping!

Jamaa's wild world of Kimbara Outback is based on a real-life wild place in Australia, the only continent occupied entirely by a single country. The Australian Outback is the vast and harsh interior wilderness of this country.

While many call the interior of the Australian continent the Outback, this vast area goes by a lot of different names. Australians are more likely to call it the bush, but it's also known as the "back of beyond," "never-never," and "back country."

The land of never-never isn't without cities! Located in the heart of the Outback is the town of Alice Springs. Tucked away in a red desert landscape, this place got its start 140 years ago as a telegraph station. It soon grew into a frontier settlement. Today, this remote town is a bustling tourist destination as people use it as a gateway for exploring the central Australian Outback. Alice Springs is also a great place to learn about pioneer history, Aboriginal culture, and to hike and explore mountain ranges, desert parks, and nature trails.

PECK

ALPHA TIP

Every pet in Jamaa does a fun trick when you click on them. Some pets, like the hummingbird and the joey, do different tricks depending on which accessories they have!

An Australian dingo patrols the Outback.

This farming fenceline stretches as far as the eye can see in southern Queensland.

The Australian Outback

The Land Down Under

THE RUGGED, RURAL OUTBACK OF Australia is known for being a land crawling with deadly snakes, dangerous crocodiles, and scorching temperatures. Few people live here. Of the more than 23 million people who call Australia home, the majority reside in cities near the coast. The 60,000 people who do live in the Outback survive by sheep and cattle ranching and mining. The native people of Australia, the Aboriginals, are nomadic hunters and gatherers.

If you believe the Outback habitat consists mostly of dry desert land, you'd be partially right. The Outback comprises many deserts. The five largest are the Great Victoria Desert, the Great Sandy Desert, the Tanami Desert, the Simpson Desert, and the Gibson Desert. But this enormous region of Australia is also home to mountain ranges, savannas, grasslands, and woodlands.

Over 15 million years ago, this area was a lush rain forest. But it began drying out, and today it features mostly hot weather and arid soil. Yet this land has a natural beauty. Red sand deserts, rock formations, hot springs, and gorges are just some of the sights people clamor to see when touring here.

The idea of the Outback being home to kangaroos is a true one, although kangaroos live in other places in Australia, not just here. The Outback is also home to the dingo, a wild dog. The largest wild camel population in the world lives here, too! They share the land with snakes, spiders, lizards, and wallabies.

Happy Hopper: Wallabies are marsupials, or pouched mammals. Their powerful hind legs give them the ability to jump long distances.

THE First AUSTRALIANS

A traditional culture

ABORIGINALS, THE NATIVE PEOPLE OF AUSTRALIA, HAD the continent to themselves for nearly 50,000 years before the establishment of the first European settlement in 1788. They're actually one of the oldest living populations in the world. Today, indigenous people make up only 3 percent of Australia's population.

Australia is a vast continent with many types of climates and terrain. The Aboriginals, who believe in living in harmony with their environment, were able to survive in rain forests, deserts, and everywhere in between. But when European colonization began to take place, many Aboriginals were killed or forced to leave their lands.

Today, Aboriginals still maintain their traditional culture. As a people influenced greatly by the natural world, their art, music, and dance reflect that as well as their spiritual beliefs.

Deadliest Animals of Australia

Saltwater Crocodile

Salties are what Australians call saltwater crocodiles, the biggest, baddest creatures found in the Outback! Salties can be aggressive, territorial, and they are known to attack humans.

Inland Taipan

Meet the most poisonous snake in the world, the inland taipan. One bite from this snake delivers enough paralyzing venom to kill 100 men! Luckily this snake rarely bites humans.

Sydney Funnel-Web Spider

The prize goes to Australia for what is likely the world's most poisonous spider! The venom of a Sydney funnel-web spider is one of the most toxic to humans of all the spider species.

Eastern Brown Snake

The Eastern brown snake is the second most toxic snake in the world, but it ranks first in Australia for causing the most snakebite deaths every year!

Redback Spider

If you're using the dunny (bathroom) in the Outback, check under the toilet seat first! The deadly redback spider likes to hide there, as well as in mailboxes and cupboards!

Tiger Snake

Pretty stripes, deadly venom! Tiger snakes get their name because of their tigerlike stripes. They cause the second highest number of snake bites in Australia.

SO YOU WANT TO BE A KOALA?

Pouch Escape: When a koala joey leaves Mom's pouch, the baby will ride on her back or cling to her belly!

Let Out Your Loudest Bellow!

YOU CAN'T TELL just by looking at a koala's adorable face, but these tree dwellers are actually one of nature's loud-mouths. Their bellows sound like a combination of an ear-rattling burp and a snore!

Eucalyptus trees provide both food and shelter for these pouched mammals, or marsupials, who spend almost all of their time searching for the tastiest leaves. But eucalyptus leaves are poisonous, tough to digest, and not very nutritious. But koalas' specially adapted digestive system extracts every drop of energy from the leaves while neutralizing their toxins, making the leaves safe to eat and healthy at the same time. Because of their diet, koalas smell a lot like cough drops!

Are You a Koala?

IF YOU'RE OFTEN THE LOUDEST VOICE IS THE ROOM, BUT ALSO LOVE TO NAP, YOU'LL ENJOY BEING A NOISY (YET ADORABLE) KOALA!

STATS

KOALA
- TYPE: Mammal
- DIET: Eucalyptus leaves
- LIFE SPAN: 20 years
- SIZE: Up to 33 inches (84 cm)
- WEIGHT: 20 pounds (9 kg)
- STATUS: Threatened
- WHERE THEY LIVE: Australia

...or a KANGAROO?

HOP to it!

TODAY, MOST PEOPLE IN THE world are familiar with these hopping marsupials that carry their babies in a pouch on their belly. Kangaroos have very big feet, which enable them to leap 30 feet (9 m) in a single bound! They can also travel at speeds of 30 miles an hour (48 kph). Their huge tails help to balance them as they leap amazing distances.

The term "kangaroo" broadly refers to a family of more than 60 species, includ-ing rat kangaroos and wal-labies. Grey kangaroos, red kangaroos, and wallaroos are referred to as the great kanga-roos because they are larger than all the other species.

STATS

RED KANGAROO

▸ TYPE: Mammal
▸ DIET: Grass, leaves, and roots
▸ LIFE SPAN: Up to 23 years
▸ SIZE: 6 feet (1.8 m) tall
▸ WEIGHT: 200 pounds (90 kg)
▸ WHERE THEY LIVE: Australia

Aussie Wildlife

Filled With Unique Creatures!

AUSTRALIA IS HOME TO SOME COOL WILDLIFE. THAT'S because Australia, surrounded by both the Pacific and Indian Oceans, is very much isolated from the rest of the world. More than 80 percent of the mammals, reptiles, plants, and frogs in Australia can be found nowhere else on the planet! If any of these animals were to disappear from Australia, they'd be extinct on Earth.

Today, 86 Australian animal species are considered critically endangered, which is the highest risk of extinction. Some of the species are small marsupials like Gilbert's potoroo, woylies, and the Kangaroo Island dunnart.

Tasmanian devils, feisty mammals famous for their scary growls, were almost wiped out as pests by farmers until they were made a protected species in 1941. They made a comeback, but a contagious illness wiped out huge numbers of the devils. Scientists are working on a cure to save this species from extinction.

Tasmanian devil

DESTINATION A.J.

MEDICAL CENTER

Kimbara Outback can be a tough place, so if you get any scrapes or bruises while exploring this rugged terrain, stop by the Medical Center! Visit the Medical Center Shop on the first floor to purchase bandages or other items you might need to patch yourself up. For more serious injuries, head up the stairs to the doctor's office!

This view of Central Australia's Ayers Rock shows its rich, red color.

Ayers Rock

A Sacred Stone

Ayers Rock

A Sacred Stone

FROM A LAND OF FLAT PLAINS rises a majestic, massive rock. Its red color almost makes you believe you've landed on a Martian landscape. Yet the largest monolith, or single stone rock, in the world is located in the middle of the Outback!

Ayers Rock, or Uluru as the Aboriginal owners of this landmark call it, can be found in Central Australia in the Uluru-Kata Tjuta National Park. This famous natural attraction rises 1,142 feet (348 m) above the plain and is 2.2 miles (3.6 km) long and 1.2 miles (1.9 km) wide. That's a big rock!

It's not only the size of Ayers Rock that makes it special. Formed more than 500 million years ago, it's made of feldspar-rich sandstone called arkose. The Aboriginals consider it a sacred place where their ancestors originated. They'll guide visitors to the base of the rock during sunrise to see the spectacular changing colors as the rays of the sun play upon it. More than 250,000 people visit Ayers Rock each year.

The national park where Uluru is found is home to more than 150 bird species and reptiles like the monitor lizard and the western brown snake. Dingoes, red kangaroos, wallaroos, and several species of bats also live here, including the Australian false vampire bat.

The next time you visit Kimbara Outback, head over to the wooden deck and check out the view. The big rock in the distance bears a striking resemblance to Uluru!

A lace monitor lizard looks out over the desert in Australia's Mungo National Park.

OUTBACK DOUBLE TAKE

see if you can spot the 10 differences between these two pictures.

spot the differences

Rock walls line this part of the Outback in Australia's Northern Territory.

Find the answers on page 233.

Extras

THE MAKING OF ANIMAL JAM
Take a peek behind the scenes!

HAVE YOU EVER WONDERED HOW YOUR FAVORITE AJ ANIMAL, PLACE, OR game was created? Take a rare look behind the scenes of Animal Jam and learn from the pros at Smart Bomb Interactive, the studio that brings the characters to life on your computer screen!

It takes more than a village to create the world of Jamaa. It's more like an army of artists! Animators, character designers, environment designers, illustrators, 3-D modelers, writers, game designers, and musicians are all needed to bring Jamaa to life. Programmers and Web designers help turn their creations into the animals and worlds you visit and play with every day!

The Origin of the Alphas and Pets

AFTER CREATING THE ANIMALS, THE NEXT big challenge for the art team was designing the Alphas. The artists drew upon movies from their childhoods—like *Thundercats, Goonies, The Lion King, The Muppets, The Secret of NIMH,* and *Star Wars*—for inspiration for the Alphas. When drawing the Alphas, Smart Bomb artists make sure their poses are strong to highlight their epicness!

Pets, on the other hand, should be the most adorable creatures you've ever seen. The art team likens Pets to marshmallows injected with sweet frosting, sprinkled with sugar. If a new Pet doesn't make players squee or cry a little with joy, it's not cute enough! Smart Bomb artists use the most basic shapes for creating Pets, called the "baby formula": a colossal head with almost no body. They must be smaller than the smallest Animal Jam animal.

Animal Art: Every Animal Jam animal goes through many rounds of sketches. Here are some you may recognize!

Animal Jam Artist Q&A

Here's how the original animals were created, according to the art team at Smart Bomb Interactive:

Creating the Animals

When the art team first started on the original sketches for the initial Animal Jam animals, they were too cute. After an extensive review, the designers knew they needed to make them look older, more like teenagers. That's when the style that players see today started to emerge. The artists decided to mute the colors and to make the animals' heads smaller. Square shapes and counter curves are the basic structure of each animal —scaly skin or fur is then added. Every animal is meant to resemble a great toy that you would want to own and display somewhere.

Making the Cut

Among the first animals the art team created were a pig and a dinosaur! Why didn't they make it into Jamaa? Smart Bomb took a poll of *National Geographic Kids* readers and asked them to pick their favorites. It was up to the players. Even now, the new animals Smart Bomb puts in the game come from player feedback. So don't rule out pigs and dinosaurs in Jamaa just yet!

The Horrid Wasteland of Frumpy Things

The bottom line: If an animal is not cool or cute or both, it does not belong in Animal Jam! But rejected designs and ideas don't just disappear. The art team keeps them all in a special place, which they jokingly call "The Horrid Wasteland of Frumpy Things"!

BUILDING JaMaa

Early Draft:
One of the first designs for Jamaa Township

CreatinG the COOLest WORLdS!

THE SUNNY SHORES OF CRYSTAL Sands, the dark Sarepia Forest, the towering heights of Mt. Shiveer. These worlds didn't exist until the Smart Bomb team created them. Now all Jammers can splash in the waves at Crystal Sands, climb the tallest trees in Sarepia Forest, and trek up snowy Mt. Shiveer.

New worlds are added to Jamaa from time to time. What's next? Keep playing wild to find out!

How are worlds created? Environment designers draw their inspiration from real-life biomes around the world. A few sketches kick-start the brainstorming, and once an idea is fully formed, it's full steam ahead! Yet even when the finished world makes its debut in Jamaa, it's still not quite done. You, the players, bring it to life by exploring and playing wild in it!

How'd They Do That?

IT'S ONE THING TO HAVE AN IDEA FOR A GREAT ANIMAL CHARACTER OR AN AWESOME new world. But how does it get from an artist's imagination to your computer screen? Technology! The team at Smart Bomb uses software programs like Adobe Photoshop, Illustrator, and Flash, as well as Autodesk Maya 3-D Animation, to create the virtual characters and worlds you know so well. Over 3,000 pictures are drawn to complete just one animal. The process takes about two and a half months.

To bring a new world to Jamaa can take from six weeks to two months. The design team builds upon the rough sketches of the environment. Once the new land is finished, they begin to test it for any bugs or glitches. They also get to play in the new world to make sure it's a fun one, where Jammers will have a blast!

216

The Beginnings of Jamaa

WHERE'S THE BEST PLACE TO PLAY WILD? In a jungle, of course!

When Smart Bomb environment designers first began to create the world of Jamaa, they needed a main place for players to land when entering the game. To capture the adventure of Jamaa, they decided on a jungle theme. In the initial concept sketches, trees were heavily featured. The designers studied rain forests around the world. They were especially inspired by Angkor Wat, an ancient city built in the tropical rain forest of Cambodia over 800 years ago. The concept changed, and ancient ruins and statues sprung up among the trees. Jamaa's Lost Temple of Zios was born!

You might be thinking that Jamaa Township, not the Lost Temple of Zios, is the central hub of Jamaa and the first place new players enter. And you're right! The design process is always changing and one idea can lead to another.

After the Lost Temple of Zios was created, the designers went to work on Jamaa Township. Their goal: create a world that looked like the animals themselves had built it. The buildings would be primitive, chunky, and more crudely assembled than you'd see in a modern, human city. No synthetic materials, like plastic, metal, or vinyl, would be used.

The finished design captured a welcoming village center with inviting storefronts—and prompted the decision to make Jamaa Township the central point from which players would embark on their adventures. After meeting with Liza on the Blue Heron, all new Jammers are dropped off in Jamaa Township.

As the designers add new worlds, they always strive to meet their key objective: to create exciting lands where Jammers can explore and experience awesome adventures!

Building Environments: Many drafts came before the final look for Temple of Zios was achieved.

Discover your ALPHa Personality!

ALL OF JAMAA'S ALPHAS are COOL, BUT THEY'RE DIFFERENT, TOO! WHO are you MOST Like?

1. What's your favorite place to visit in Jamaa?

a. Jamaa Township (+6 pts.)
b. Kimbara Outback (+5 pts.)
c. Lost Temple of Zios (+4 pts.)
d. Coral Canyons (+3 pts.)
e. Appondale (+2 pts.)
f. Sarepia Forest (+1 pt.)

2. Out of the following, what's your favorite hobby?

a. Photography (+6 pts.)
b. Gardening (+5 pts.)
c. Magic tricks (+4 pts.)
d. Arts and crafts (+3 pts.)
e. Reading (+2 pts.)
f. Traveling (+1 pt.)

3. Which den in Jamaa would you most like to live in?

a. Princess Castle, so there will be plenty of room for my friends to visit (+6 pts.)
b. Tree House (+5 pts.)
c. Doesn't matter, as long as I have room for my workshop (+4 pts.)
d. Enchanted Hollow (+3 pts.)
e. Castle (+2 pts.)
f. Volcano (+1 pt.)

4. You're hungry. What do you snack on?

a. Celery sticks (+6 pts.)
b. Salad (+5 pts.)
c. A banana (+4 pts.)
d. Carrots (+3 pts.)
e. Steak (+2 pts.)
f. A cheeseburger (+1 pt.)

5. Which word best describes you?

a. Sympathetic (+6 pts.)
b. Fun-loving (+5 pts.)
c. Inventive (+4 pts.)
d. Creative (+3 pts.)
e. Polite (+2 pts.)
f. Quiet (+1 pt.)

6. Out of the following, which do you dislike the most?

a. Friends fighting (+6 pts.)
b. People not recycling (+5 pts.)
c. Tasks or projects that are too easy to do (+4 pts.)
d. Boredom (+3 pts.)
e. Being left out (+2 pts.)
f. Crowds (+1 pt.)

7. It's your birthday and a wrapped present is sitting in front of you. You hope it's:

a. A camera (+6 pts.)
b. A new plant for your garden (+5 pts.)
c. Tools (+4 pts.)
d. Art supplies (+3 pts.)
e. A book (+2 pts.)
f. Camping gear (+1 pt.)

Add up your points!

Liza

Cosmo

36–42 points: You're most like Liza the panda! You're a terrific friend who always wants to help others.

30–35 points: You're most like Cosmo the koala! You're a nature lover who likes to spend time outside.

Graham

Peck

24–29 points: You're most like Graham the monkey! You enjoy a challenge and like to tinker with tools.

18–23 points: You're most like Peck the bunny! You're a creative spirit who always needs to be doing something fun and exciting.

Sir Gilbert

Greely

12–17 points: You're most like Sir Gilbert the tiger! You're always on the lookout to meet new and interesting people.

7–11 points: You're most like Greely the wolf! You're quiet but that doesn't mean you're shy; you just need your alone time.

PLACES
iN JaMaa

IF YOU COULD PiCK tHE PERFECT PLACE FOR YOU iN JaMaa BASED ON YOUR PERSONALitY, WHERE WOULD it BE?

> If these don't match you, don't worry, it's just for fun!

1. If I'm out in the sun, I:

a. Look for the nearest building to take cover (+4 pts.)

b. Soak it up—I love the feel of the sun on my skin. (+1 pt.)

c. Search for a shady tree to sit under (+2 pts.)

d. Find a pool or body of water to dive into (+3 pts.)

2. To me, the most calming place to be is:

a. A quiet spot surrounded by trees (+2 pts.)

b. A place where there are lots of other people around because I don't like being lonely (+4 pts.)

c. An open place where the sky seems to go on forever (+1 pt.)

d. Anywhere I can swim (+3 pts.)

3. Spiders and snakes make you react this way:

a. Freak out! (+4 pts.)

b. I don't love them, but I can deal with them. (+3 pts.)

c. Spiders and snakes? Where? Can I have one? (+1 pt.)

d. If I see one, I'll jot a note of it in my nature journal. (+2 pts.)

4. Your perfect party would be:

a. A beach party (+3 pts.)

b. A picnic in the woods (+2 pts.)

c. In a restaurant (+4 pts.)

d. A rock climbing party (+1 pt.)

5. The best way to get around is:

a. In a four-wheel drive truck (+1 pt.)

b. On a bicycle (+4 pts.)

c. In a boat (+3 pts.)

d. On foot (+2 pts.)

6. When you travel around Jamaa, you spend most of your time:

a. Shopping (+4 pts.)
b. Exploring the forests (+2 pts.)
c. Playing in the mud (+1 pt.)
d. Exploring the ocean (+3 pts.)

7. My feelings about rainy days can be summed up like this:

a. They are a great excuse to curl up with a book. (+2 pts.)
b. I'm inside a lot so it doesn't really matter to me if it's raining or not. (+4 pts.)
c. I love getting wet so no problem! (+3 pts.)
d. The worst. I need sunshine! (+1 pt.)

Add up your points!

7–11 points:
Your perfect Jamaa place is a desertlike area like Coral Canyons, Kimbara Outback, or Appondale!
As long as you have the sun on your face and the wind in your hair, you're a happy camper!

12–17 points:
Your perfect Jamaa place is Sarepia Forest or the Lost Temple of Zios!
You need trees and lots of them to be happy, so these wooded areas are a great place for you to hang out.

18–22 points:
Your perfect Jamaa place is any of the oceans, like Kani Cove, Bahari Bay, Deep Blue, or Crystal Reef!
You were born to swim and splash, and in Jamaa you can do that every day!

23–28 points:
Your perfect Jamaa place is Jamaa Township!
Plenty of shopping and plenty of buddies will ensure you're never bored!

WE ALL HAVE DAYS WHEN WE WANT TO UNLEASH THE ANIMAL WITHIN!
DISCOVER YOUR HIDDEN ANIMAL PERSONALITY.

FIND YOUR

1. You've been invited to a costume party. What do you wear?

a. A costume of my favorite cartoon character (+4 pts.)
b. A cute and adorable animal costume (+3 pts.)
c. Something funny. I want everyone to laugh when I walk in the door. (+2 pts.)
d. Whatever's the scariest! (+1 pt.)

2. Gym class today. You've got your fingers crossed that you'll be able to:

a. Sit in the stands and cheer on your friends (+4 pts.)
b. Practice your cartwheels (+3 pts.)
c. Run a relay race with your buddies (+2 pts.)
d. Play dodgeball (+1 pt.)

3. You're invited to a campout in the woods. You're:

a. A little nervous to be away from home for the night (+4 pts.)
b. Okay as long as you've got plenty of friends to keep you company (+3 pts.)
c. Excited! I'll stay up all night talking to my friends. (+2 pts.)
d. Up for the challenge—if any trouble comes your way, you'll be ready for it! (+1 pt.)

4. You heard your teacher talking about a field trip. You're hoping your class will:

a. Visit a museum (+4 pts.)
b. Go to a toy store (+3 pts.)
c. It doesn't matter as long as I'm with my friends! (+2 pts.)
d. Play laser tag (+1 pt.)

5. You're invited to a friend's birthday party. For a gift, you give him or her a:

a. Copy of your favorite book (+4 pts.)
b. Stuffed animal (+3 pts.)
c. Friendship bracelet (+2 pts.)
d. Football (+1 pt.)

6. Your idea of a great pet is a:

a. Dog (+4 pts.)
b. Hamster (+3 pts.)
c. Parrot (+2 pts.)
d. Snake (+1 pt.)

If these don't match you, don't worry, it's just for fun!

WILD SIDE!

7. Whenever your friends are feeling down, you cheer them up by:

a. Listening to them talk about how they are feeling (+4 pts.)
b. Giving them a hug (+3 pts.)
c. Making them laugh (+2 pts.)
d. Helping them fix their problem (+1 pt.)

8. Which of these personality traits do you like the least?

a. Untrustworthiness (+4 pts.)
b. Meanness (+3 pts.)
c. Snobbishness (+2 pts.)
d. Cowardice (+1 pt.)

9. What kind of books do you like to read?

a. Nonfiction—I like to learn about the world around me. (+4 pts.)
b. Fairy tales (+3 pts.)
c. Anything funny! (+2 pts.)
d. Action and adventure (+1 pt.)

10. You're hungry. You reach for:

a. An apple (+4 pts.)
b. Carrot sticks (+3 pts.)
c. Candy (+2 pts.)
d. A hamburger (+1 pt.)

Add up your points!

10–17 points:
You are a ferocious animal!
Uh-oh. We don't want to make you mad. Because your personality quiz results reveal you're the most like some of the toughest (and toothiest) animals out there, like sharks, crocodiles, wolves, and tigers.

18–25 points:
You are a friendly animal!
Like monkeys and dolphins, your social group is important to you, and you always make time for your friends. Everyone looks to you to cheer them up when they are feeling down.

26–33 points:
You are a happy animal!
You bring a happy smile wherever you go! We bet you've got a poster hanging in your room of at least one of these cuddly animals: bunny, koala, panda, raccoon, or penguin.

34–40 points:
You are a loyal animal!
Gentle and strong, you are a loyal friend and family member. When times are hard, everyone knows they can count on you to pull through. Just a few of the animals that remind us of you are elephants and giraffes.

TEST YOUR ANIMAL JAM IQ!

HAVE YOU BEEN PAYING ATTENTION? SEE IF YOU ARE A JAMAA EXPERT!

1. What day of the week is a super-rare item for sale in one of the shops in Jamaa?

a. Tuesday
b. Saturday
c. Monday
d. Friday

2. The Chamber of Knowledge can be found in which land of Jamaa?

a. Jamaa Township
b. Lost Temple of Zios
c. Appondale
d. Coral Canyons

3. What did the Phantoms steal that caused many animal species to disappear from Jamaa?

a. Heartstones
b. Gems
c. The statue of Zios
d. Diamonds

4. When you prepare to go on an Adventure, which Alpha trains you?

a. Liza
b. Cosmo
c. Greely
d. Peck

5. The statue found in Jamaa Township is of:

a. Zios
b. Sir Gilbert

c. Mira
d. An arctic wolf

6. In which land of Jamaa can you find the humpback whale for your Journey Book?

a. Crystal Reef
b. Deep Blue
c. Kani Cove
d. Mt. Shiveer

7. Jammers can have how many buddies on their Buddy List?

a. 1,000
b. 100
c. 50
d. 250

8. The game in which you recycle items to earn Gems is called:

a. Phantom's Treasure
b. Overflow
c. Super Sort
d. Double Up

9. Disc Toss is a game you can play with which pet?

a. Duck
b. Snake
c. Puppy
d. Butterfly

10. Who has a laboratory in the Lost Temple of Zios?

a. Gilbert the tiger Alpha

b. Brady Barr
c. Tierney Thys
d. Cosmo the koala Alpha

11. Greely the Alpha is a:

a. Wolf
b. Tiger
c. Bunny
d. Panda

12. Which of the following is NOT a pet in Jamaa?

a. Raccoon
b. Shark
c. Fox
d. Jellyfish

Find the answers on **PAGE 233**.

Games in Jamaa

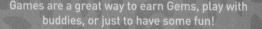
Games are a great way to earn Gems, play with buddies, or just to have some fun!

Play dress-up for a chance to win Gems in Best Dressed! Choose the colors and wardrobe you think best match the theme and strut your stuff on the stage. If other Jammers like your look, they'll vote for you. If you get a lot of votes, you can win lots of Gems! Find this game in Coral Canyons. There's even an ocean version especially for ocean animals in Bahari Bay.

Have you always wanted a chemistry set to experiment with? Dr. Brady Barr will let you borrow his anytime you want. Just stop by his lab in the Lost Temple of Zios.

For the cost of five Gems, you can try your luck at winning a plushie from one of the many Claw Machines located around Jamaa, including Appondale, Sarepia Forest, and Crystal Sands.

The animals are hiding in their holes. Can you find them by matching up pairs of tigers, bunnies, pandas, and birds? Go to Crystal Sands to start making animal matches.

Nom nom nom! Find out what it's like to be part of the ocean food chain in this eat-or-be-eaten game. Feast on smaller fish but avoid the bigger fish who'd like to make a meal out of you. Dive into Crystal Reef to start chomping.

The sky is falling! Actually, it's even worse than that. Nasty Phantoms are erupting from a volcano, and it's up to you and five other Jammers to avoid the falling Phantoms and last as long as you can without being hit by one. The last Jammer standing wins! Start running for cover in the Lost Temple of Zios.

The Phantoms are hiding out in forts, and it's up to you, your trusty slingshot, and some fruit to save the day! Once you destroy all the Phantoms in a fort you move on to the next level. Different types of fruit can do different damage to the forts and the Phantoms, so pay attention. Go to Appondale to start flinging fruit.

In this pinball-like game, you shoot balls. Depending on where your ball lands, you'll earn Gems. Try to shoot the ball into the face of Zios. It will light up. If you light up all three suns you'll earn a Gem bonus! This game can be found in the Chamber of Knowledge in the Lost Temple of Zios.

Match Gems to knock them down and to clear Phantoms who are trapped in the ice. If you break five or more Gems you'll create a combo and earn bonus points! This icy game is in Mt. Shiveer.

Meet the hungry, hungry hedgehog! He needs to gobble up as many berries as he can. Guide him through the maze, but watch out for those pesky Phantoms. If the hedgehog gobbles up

a special crystal, he can turn the table on the Phantoms and catch them. Head over to Sarepia Forest to start playing.

And they're off! Race to the finish line against five other Jammers in this fast-paced game. But watch out for any obstacles in your way. You'll need to jump over them in order to stay in the lead. If you have a horse, you'll automatically play as that when you go into the game. If not, one will be provided for you. Start your day at the races in Jamaa Township.

How far can an armadillo go? Find out in Long Shot! Fling the armadillo as far as you can to earn Gems. If you land your armadillo on geysers or moles, you'll get an extra burst of speed that will take it even farther. This game is in Coral Canyons.

What Mira says goes! Watch the pattern of colors and sounds, then try to copy them. The more you match, the longer (and harder!) the pattern gets. The faster you duplicate the pattern, the more Gems you will earn. Test your copying skills in the Chamber of Knowledge in the Lost Temple of Zios.

Make a moat around your sand castle in Overflow! Connect the paths to your castle so the water will flow. The longer the path, the more Gems you will earn. Have fun digging in the sand at Crystal Sands.

Pet Games
Some games in Jamaa can only be played with a pet. They are:
DISC TOSS – Puppy
DUCKY DASH – Duck
SSSSSNAKE – Snake
PET WASH – Can be played with any pet!

A swarm of angry insects is headed your way. The only way to stop them is to strategically place animals that love to eat bugs—like snakes, frogs, and lizards—in their path. If you let an insect escape, your health will be damaged. Bring on the bug control in Appondale.

Evil Phantoms are flying high above Jamaa and threatening this land's peaceful existence! Grab a spaceship to stop them. The tricky red Phantoms will need to be hit more than once to defeat them. Play Phantom Fighter in Club Geoz in Jamaa Township.

Food Games

Throughout Jamaa are places where you can make a snack for yourself. Grab some buttery popcorn at the **POPCORN MACHINE,** a warm cup of cocoa at the **HOT COCOA MACHINE,** or a refreshing smoothie at the **SMOOTHIE MACHINE.**

In this game, which can be found in Sol Arcade in Jamaa Township, you have just one shot to take down the Phantom ship. If you win, you'll get a cool toy for your den! It costs 10 Gems to play this game.

Search for the hidden treasures in the picture. The faster you find them, the more Gems you'll get. If you get stuck, use a hint. But if you can figure out where the treasure is hiding without using hints, you'll get a bonus! Swim to the very bottom of Deep Blue to start your treasure hunt.

Shoot pill bugs from a tulip to clear the screen of ladybugs and earn Gems. Each time you clear a level you'll learn a fun fact about pill bugs. If you have any leftover pill bugs you'll score a bonus! Bug out over this game in Sarepia Forest.

Hop in a boat and take part in an exciting river race in Jamaa Township. You can race solo or against other Jammers. Shoot for the arrows and they'll give your boat a boost of speed, but avoid rocks and whirlpools. Cross the finish line first to win a Gem bonus!

Located at the top of Coral Canyons is one of the most popular games in Jamaa: Sky High. Bounce off the clouds and soar through the air as you collect Gems. If you can bounce your way to the very top and reach the treasure chest, you'll win a special rare item!

Spiders have invaded the trees of Jamaa. Help stop them by zapping spiders in Club Geoz in Jamaa Township. Zapping more spiders earns you more Gems. Zap every spider in a round to earn a Gem bonus!

Test your skills in Bahari Bay as you race your dolphin to the finish line. Be sure to avoid all obstacles or you'll slow down. If you have a dolphin, you'll play as that. If not, you'll get a loaner dolphin for the duration of the race.

Recycling is a supercool thing to do. When you do it in Sarepia Forest while playing Super Sort, you can even earn Gems!

Sort the items into their correct recycling bins. If you sort them all without making a mistake you'll get a Gem bonus!

Calling all smarties! Put your knowledge about animals and our planet to the test by playing a round of the challenging Temple of Trivia in the Lost Temple of Zios. Compete against other Jammers by answering the multiple-choice questions. The quicker you answer, the more Gems you'll win!

Head to the eagle's nest in Coral Canyons to play Swoopy Eagle! Use your mouse or the space bar to flap your wings and soar through the cacti. Just be careful not to touch any part of the cacti—especially the spines!

When you visit Tierney's Aquarium in Crystal Sands, you can discover exotic marine animals, learn facts, and win awesome prizes! Touch different creatures long enough to fill the timer. Fill your Touch Pool log to earn cool prizes.

Located on the Canyons Pathway that connects Coral Canyons to Crystal Sands, Twister is a game where you help a bird escape a tornado! Avoid buildings and flying debris to escape the twister. Fly through the rings to get a score bonus.

Take a relaxing parachute ride down to the ground as you collect Gems. Wait—we forgot to mention the Phantoms! They'll get in your way and try to take your Gems from you. If you can reach the ground without hitting a Phantom you'll get a Gem bonus! Climb to the top of the trees in Sarepia Forest to play this game.

THE RULES

There are rules everywhere to keep people safe.

When you're riding in a car, you have to put your seat belt on. If you're riding a bike, you wear a helmet. Even extreme sports—like bungee jumping and skydiving—are done with strict safety guidelines.

Going on the Internet is no different. There are rules you need to follow to keep yourself and others safe. Animal Jam and its creators are committed to providing a safe environment so everyone can have a fun gaming experience. Here are four tips you should always remember online, whether you're on Animal Jam or any other website.

PLAY WILD, PLAY SAFE

1. **BE VERY CAREFUL WHO YOU SHARE YOUR PERSONAL INFORMATION WITH, LIKE YOUR REAL NAME AND AGE.**
Keep your contact info, like your phone number and home and email addresses, private. Only share when your parents say it's okay to share.

2. **NEVER GIVE ANYONE YOUR PASSWORD.**
Passwords for any sites, not just Animal Jam, should be kept to yourself and your parents. People online might promise to give you cool stuff if you give them your password. Don't believe them. It's a trick!

3. **SOMETIMES PEOPLE AREN'T WHO THEY SAY THEY ARE ONLINE.**
Never meet anyone in person who you met on the Internet.

4. **BE NICE TO EVERYONE.**
Do you like having fun on Animal Jam? We do too! Let's keep it a happy place by being nice to everyone. When people are mean or bully each other, it makes the Internet less fun. So do your part and always be friendly.

Follow these rules online to stay safe and keep having a good time! For more information on Animal Jam's safety and privacy policies, grab a parent and check out: www.animaljam.com/rules and www.animaljam.com/privacy.

ANSWER KEY

Pages 78–79
Lost Temple of Zios

Pages 94–95
Appondale

Pages 110–111
Sarepia Forest

Pages 126–127
Coral Canyons

1-c, 2-a, 3-True, 4-b, 5-True, 6-False, 7-d, 8-d, 9-b, 10-c

Pages 150–151
Bahari Bay

Pages 162–163
Crystal Reef

Pages 174–175
Kani Cove

Pages 184–185
Deep Blue

1-c, 2-b, 3-a, 4-True, 5-b, 6-d, 7-a, 8-False, 9-c, 10-True, 11-False, 12-a, 13-True, 14-d, 15-b

Pages 210–211
Kimbara Outback

Page 224
Animal Jam IQ

1-c, 2-b, 3-a, 4-a, 5-c, 6-a, 7-b, 8-c, 9-c, 10-b, 11-a, 12-b

INDEX BOLDFACE INDICATES ILLUSTRATIONS

235

ILLUSTRATION CREDITS

Cover Image © Chris Harris/SuperStock; 26 (UPLE), © Jason Kasumovic/SS; 26 (LOLE), © Janelle Lugge/SS; 26 (RT), © edella/SS; 28 (UP), © Gnel Karapetyan/DRT; 29 (UPLE), © Fabrice Coffrini/AFP/GI/Newscom; 29 (UPRT), © Manjunath Kiran/EPA/Newscom; 29 (CTR LE), © Fred Ward/CO; 29 (CTR RT), © PoodlesRock/CO; 29 (LOLE), © Hilary Morgan/AL; 35 (UPRT), © Underwood & Underwood/CO; 35 (UPLE), © Hulton-Deutsch Collection/CO; 35 (LOLE), NASA; 35 (LOLE), Brady Barr; 35 (LORT), Mike Johnson/NGC; 37 (LOCTR), © AP Photo/Cecil Whig, Adelma Gregory-Bunnel; 37 (UP), Courtesy of Gary A. Rohde; 37 (UP CTR), © ED Jones/AFP/GI/Newscom; 37 (LORT), © Joanne Lefson39 (LE), © sittipong/SS; 39 (UPRT), NAS/Photo Researchers/GI; 39 (LORT), Hulton Archive/GI; 40 (LORT), © Gea Strucks/DRT; 43 (UPLE), © Mgkuijpers/DRT; 43 (UPRT), © Volodymyr Byrdyak/DRT; 43 (LOLE), © Alanjeffery/DRT; 43 (LORT), © Juniors Bildarchiv GmbH/AL; 44 (LE), © Johan W. Elzenga/SS; 44 (CTR), © rashworth/SS; 44 (RT), © Maslov Dmitry/SS; 47 (UP), © Brown/GTphoto; 47 (LOLE), © Noah Goodrich/CATERS NEWS; 47,(LORT) © Karine Aigner; 49 (LO), © Andresr/SS; 51 (UP), © Reuters/Thomas ; 51 (CTR), © Donna Kassewitz/SpeakDolphin; 51 (LO), Dean Pomerleau; 53 (UP), © Juniors Bildarchiv GmbH/AL; 53 (INSET), © Mark Moffett/Minden Pictures; 53 (LO), © Phil Crosby/AL; 56 (UP), © leungchopan/SS; 56 (UPRT), © Kwiktor/DRT; 56 (LORT), © David Coleman/DRT; 56 (BACK), © IR Stone/SS; 57 (UPLE), © Roberto Marinello/DRT; 57 (UPRT), © Simon Hack/DRT; 57 (LO), © Typhoonski/DRT; 58 (CTR), © Scattoselvaggio/DRT; 59 (CTR), © nikkytok/SS; 60 (UP), © Justpeachy/DRT; 60 (LO), © Rob Hyrons/SS; 61 (CTR), © Michael Flippo/DRT; 62 (UPLE), © ssguy/SS; 63 (UPLE), © Mike Clarke/AFP/Newscom; 63 (UPRT), Tim Flach/GI; 63 (UPLE), ROX/rox.co.uk; 63 (CTR RT), © WENN/Newscom; 63 (LOLE), © Joffet Emmanuel/Sipa; 63 (LORT), © Reuters/Toru Hanai; 64 (LOLE), © Eric Isselee/SS; 65 (LOLE), Dr_harry/DRT; 65 (LOLE), © Hilton Kotze/DRT; 68 (LOLE), Brady Barr; 68 (UPRT), © Dr Morley Read/SS; 68 (LORT), © Robyn Mackenzie/SS; 69 (UPLE), Robert Clark/NGC; 69 (UPRT), © incamerastock/AL; 69 (LO), © Peter Adams Photography Ltd/AL; 70 (UP), Don Johnston/GI; 71 (CTR), Aditya Singh/GI; 71 (LORT), © Nick Biemans/SS; 72 (BACK), © jarnbeer19/SS; 73 (UPLE), © holbox/SS; 73 (UPRT), © f9photos/SS; 73 (LO), © Vadim Petrakov/SS; 74 (BACK), © 2009fotofriends/SS; 74 (LOLE), © Palko72/DRT; 74 (CTR), © Edurivero/DRT; 75 (CTR LE), © Anton_Ivanov/SS; 75 (LOLE), © Dirk Ercken/DRT; 75 (LORT), © Anton_Ivanov/SS; 76 (CTR), © szefei/SS; 76 (UP), © Morley Read/DRT; 76 (CTR RT), © Kjersti Joergensen/DRT; 76 (CTR LE), © Dirk Ercken/SS; 76 (LO), © Larry Larsen/AL; 77 (CTR), © Roland Seitre/NPL; 78, Rebecca Hale/NGS Staff; 82 (UP), © Ekawrecker/DRT; 82 (CTR RT), Frans Lanting/NGC; 82 (LO), © Taiga/SS; 83 (LO), © Donald Sawvel/SS; 83 (UPLE), © Ajn/DRT; 83 (UPRT), © Ramblingman/DRT; 83 (LO), © Curt Wiler/AL; 84 (CTR), © Suzi Eszterhas/NPL; 85 (LO), © Peter Blackwell/NPL; 86 (CTR), © piotr_pabijan/SS; 86 (LOLE), © Eric Isselee/SS; 86 (LOCTR), © Dimijana/SS; 86 (UPRT), © Brendan van Son/SS; 86 (LORT), © Lynn M. Stone/NPL; 87 (UP CTR LE), Adam Jones/GI; 87 (LOLE), Beverly Joubert/NGC; 87 (UPLE), © Christopher Scott/AL; 87 (LO CTR LE), © Eric Gevaert/SS; 87 (UPRT), © Ramblingman/DRT; 87 (UP CTR), © Peter Wollinga/DRT; 87 (LOCTR), © Isselee/DRT; 87 (INSET), © tovovan/SS; 88 (CTR), Frans Lanting/NGC; 89 (CTR), © Tony Heald/NPL; 90 (CTR), © Byelikova/DRT; 91 (CTR), © Tudorish/DRT; 91 (LOLE), © Andries Alberts/DRT; 92 (UP), © Aurora Photos/AL; 92 (LO), © David Woodfall/NPL; 93 (LO), © Jouan & Rius/NPL; 93 (UP), © Jim Parkin/AL; 94 (CTR), © Igor Janicek/SS; 98 (BACK), © pani/SS; 98 (CTR RT), © BMJ/SS; 98 (UP), © un.bolovan/SS; 99 (UPLE), Phil Schermeister/NGC; 99 (LO), © Tom Reichner/SS; 99 (UPRT), Jordan Siemens/GI; 100 (UPLE), Jim and Jamie Dutcher/NGC; 101 (LO), Jim and Jamie Dutcher/NGC; 101 (UP), © Top-Pics TBK/AL; 101 (BACK), © Sedthachai stock/SS; 102 (CTR), © Tischenko Irina/SS; 103 (LOCTR), © age fotostock/AL; 103 (UP CTR), © Matt Freedman/DanitaDelimont/Newscom; 103 (LORT), © Robin Weaver/AL; 103 (UPRT), © Francisco Javier Gil Oreja/DRT; 104 (CTR), © Tom Reichner/SS; 105, © Gerald A. DeBoer/SS; 106 (UP), © Christian Ziegler/Minden Pictures/CO; 106 (LO), © quebecfoto/AL; 107 (LO), Brian J Skerry/NGC; 107 (UP), © Mike Grandmaison/All Canada Photos/CO; 108 (BACK), © Neale Clark/CO; 109 (CTR RT), © P.Burghardt/SS; 110 (BACK), © Ynamaku/DRT; 111 (INSET), © Sharpshot/DRT; 111 (INSET), © Daria Rybakova/DRT; 111 (INSET), © Isselee/DRT; 111 (INSET), © Dule964/DRT; 111 (INSET), © Pumba1/DRT; 111 (INSET), © Bluehand/DRT; 111 (INSET), © Natis76/DRT; 111 (INSET), © Michael Flippo/DRT; 111 (INSET), © Sirfujiyama/DRT; 111 (INSET), © Stockdreams/DRT; 114 (BACK), © amadedeus/SS; 114 (UP CTR), © Danita Delimont/AL; 114 (LORT), © Americanspirit/DRT; 114 (LOLE), © William Michael Norton/DRT; 115 (LOLE), © Mike P Shepherd/AL; 115 (UPRT), © apdesign/SS; 115 (UPLE), © Michael Elliott/DRT; 116 (BACK), © Colin Harris/era-images/AL; 117 (LOLE), © Hemis/AL; 118 (CTR), © Kenny Williams/AL; 119 (CTR), © Pim Leijen/SS; 120 (BACK), © Horizon International Images Limited/AL; 121 (UPRT), © Aurora Photos/AL; 121 (UPLE), © Karenwinton/DRT; 122 (CTR), © Nico Smit/DRT; 123 (CTR), © Maria Itina/DRT; 124

(BACK), © Miloslav Doubrava/DRT; 124 (UPLE), © Amwu/DRT; 124 (UP CTR), © Graham Hatherley/NPL; 124 (LOCTR), © Luiz Claudio Marigo/NPL; 124 (LO), © Sunheyy/DRT; 125 (LOLE), John Burcham/NGC; 126 (BACK), © Orgus88/SS; 126 (UPLE), © Ashukaili/DRT; 126 (LOLE), © Vadim Petrakov; 126 (LORT), © Umberto Shtanzman/SS; 126 (LORT), © Rich Carey/SS; 127 (UPRT), © Eric Isselee/SS; 127 (CTR), © OkPic/SS; 127 (CTR), © ajt/SS; 127 (UPLE), © Vladyslav Starozhylov/SS; 127 (LOLE), © Potapov Alexander/SS; 130 (UPRT), © stevehullphotography/SS; 130 (UP CTR), © Stephen Frink Collection/AL; 130 (LOLE), © Sandra Van Der Steen/DRT; 130 (BACK), © Ron Dale/SS; 131 (UP), © Oleg Znamenskiy/DRT; 131 (CTR), © Juniors Bildarchiv GmbH/AL; 132 (CTR), © Ioana Grecu/DRT; 133 (CTR), © Christian Musat/SS; 134 (BACK), © Ana Del Castillo/DRT; 134 (LORT), © Konstantin Kulikov/AL; 135 (UP), © Kim Taylor/NPL; 135 (LOCTR), © Chris Gotz/SS; 135 (LORT), © RGB Ventures LLC dba SuperStock/AL; 135 (LOCTR), Thomas Ames Jr./Visuals Unlimited, Inc./GI; 135 (UP CTR), Harry Rogers/GI; 136 (BACK), © bikeriderlondon/SS; 137 (UP), © Simon Gurney/DRT; 137 (LO), © Ian Wilson/DRT; 137 (BACK), © Moose Henderson/DRT; 139 (UP), Sylvain Cordier/GI; 139 (LO), Wayne Lynch/GI; 140 (LOLE), © Isselee/DRT; 141 (LOLE), © Tommiddleton/DRT; 141 (LOLE), © Isselee/DRT; 144 (BACK), © Sundari/SS; 144 (CTR RT), © Ahmad Faizal Yahya/SS; 144 (UP), © CreativeNature.nl/SS; 145 (UPRT), Win Initiative/GI; 145 (LO), © SW_Stock/SS; 145 (UPLE), © Mechanik/SS; 146 (BACK), Markus Fleute/GI; 147 (LO), © kropic1/SS; 147 (UPRT), © kropic1/SS; 147 (UPLE), © wim claes/SS; 148 (UPLE), © Jurgen Freund/NPL; 148 (BACK), Niroot Sampan/GI; 149 (CTR RT), Brady Barr; 150 (BACK), Rebecca Drobis/NGS Staff; 154 (CTR), Predrag Vuckovic/GI; 154 (UP), © KKG Photo/SS; 155 (UPRT), © Martin Maun/DRT; 155 (UPLE), © Predrag Vuckovic/GI; 156 (BACK), © Irochka/DRT; 156 (LE), © Jamiegodson/DRT; 157 (UPRT), © Song Heming/DRT; 157 (UP CTR), © Deborah Coles/DRT; 157 (CTR RT), © Amilevin/DRT; 157 (LOCTR), Mauricio Handler/NGC; 157 (LO), © Howard Chew/DRT; 157 (LOLE), © Images & Stories/AL; 158 (BACK), © Richard Carey/DRT; 159 (LO), Jason Edwards/NGC; 160 (BACK), © Michael Patrick O'Neill/AL; 160 (CTR), Mark Webster/Lonely Planet Images/GI; 161 (UPLE), © Michael Patrick O'Neill/AL; 161 (LO), © Craig Ruaux/AL; 161 (UPRT), © Alex Mustard/NPL; 162, Jeff Hunter/GI; 166 (CTR), Goldenarts/SS; 166 (UP CTR LE), © Olga Khoroshunova/DRT; 166 (UPRT), © Liquid Productions, LLC/SS; 166 (CTR RT), © Ofer Ketter/SeaPics.com; 166 (LOLE), © Jeff Rotman/AL; 167 (UPLE), Emory Kristof/NGC; 167 (UPRT), Emory Kristof/National Geographic; 167 (LO), Bruce Dale/NGC; 167 (LO), © H Bedford Lemere/English Heritage/CO; 168 (LOLE), © AP Photo/Florida Keys News Bureau, Sharon Wiley; 168 (BACK), © Sergey Dubrov/SS; 168 (LORT), © OME/Polaris/Newscom; 168 (UP CTR), © EPA/Cardiff University/Newscom; 169 (UPRT), © Lebrecht Music and Arts Photo Library/AL; 169

(LOCTR), © Ray Fairall/ZUMAPRESS/Newscom; 169 (LOLE), © Jonathan Nackstrand/AFP/GI/Newscom; 169 (CTR LE), © CO; 170 (BACK), Luis Javier Sandoval/GI; 171 (UPRT), © Masa Ushioda/SeaPics.com; 171 (CTR RT), Image Source/GI; 172 (BACK), © Alvov/SS; 173 (UPRT), © Hugoht/DRT; 174,(CTR) Rebecca Hale/NGS Staff178 (BACK), © Klara Viskova/SS; 178 (LOLE), © Richard Carey/DRT; 178 (UP), © Jeff Rotman/AL; 179 (UPLE), © Wim van Egmond/Visuals Unlimited/CO; 179 (UPRT), © Jurgen Freund/NPL; 180 (BACK), © Martin Strmiska/AL; 180 (LORT), © Sue Daly/NPL; 181 (LORT), © Planctonvideo/DRT; 182 (LORT), © David Shale/NPL; 182 (CTR), © David Shale/NPL; 183 (LORT), © Doc White/NPL; 183 (UPLE), NOAA; 183 (LOCTR), © Amanda Cotton/AL; 183 (UPRT), © Dr. Ken MacDonald/Science Source; 183 (LOLE), © David Shale/NPL; 184 (UP), © Krzysztof Odziomek/DRT; 184 (LO), © Navarone/DRT; 185 (UP), © Corina Daniela Obertas/Dreamstim; 185 (LOLE), © Anthony Hathaway/DRT; 188 (BACK), © Malchev/SS; 188 (UP), © Martin Harvey/AL; 188 (CTR LE), © Kodym/DRT; 188 (CTR RT), © Mircea Costina/DRT; 188 (LORT), © Lukas Blazek/DRT; 189 (UPRT), Andy Bardon/NGC; 189 (UPLE), © Leo & Mandy Dickinson/NPL; 189 (LOLE), © Everett Collection Inc/AL; 190 (BACK), © Robert Palmer/SS; 190 (UPLE), © Ron Niebrugge/AL; 192 (LOLE), © Rinus Baak/DRT; 192 (LO CTR RT), © Anibal Trejo/DRT; 192 (LO CTR RT), © Robert Preston Photography/AL; 192 (LORT), © Erika J Mitchell/SS; 192 (BACK), © old apple/SS; 194 (LOLE), Pete Ryan/NGC; 194 (BACK), © imagebroker/AL; 196 (BACK), © Dchauy/SS; 196 (LOCTR), © Albert Ziganshin/SS; 197 (UPLE), © Eric Baccega/NPL; 197 (LOLE), © Eric Baccega/NPL; 197 (LORT), © BMJ/SS; 198 (LOLE), © Ron Kimball/Kimball Stock; 199 (LOLE), © Howard Sandler/SS; 199 (LOLE), © nialat/SS; 202 (BACK), © Seita/Shuttersock; 202 (UPLE), © David Wall/AL; 202 (UPRT), © Itobiwan/DRT; 203 (UPLE), © John Carnemolla/SS; 203 (LORT), © Ben Mcleish/DRT; 203 (UPRT), © Travelling-light/DRT; 204 (LOCTR), © Robert Valentic/NPL; 204 (BACK), © Wildlight Photo Agency/AL; 204 (LOLE), © Brandon Cole Marine Photography/AL; 204 (LORT), © Roland Seitre/NPL; 205 (LORT), © Robert Valentic/NPL; 205 (LOLE), © Robert Valentic/NPL; 205 (LOCTR), © Graphic Science/AL; 206 (CTR), © Andras Deak/DRT; 207 (CTR), © imagebroker/AL; 209 (UPRT), © imagebroker/AL; 209 (LORT), © blickwinkel/AL; 209 (BACK), © Roland Seitre/NPL; 210 (BACK), © tommaso lizzul/SS; 211 (LORT), © Konart/DRT; 211 (LOCTR), © Engraver/DRT; 211 (UPLE), © Bahadir Yeniceri/DRT; 211 (LOLE), © Joanne Zh/DRT; 211 (LOCTR), © Lightzoom/DRT; 211 (UP CTR), © Isselee/DRT; 211 (CTR), © Isselee/DRT; 211 (LO CTR LE), © Vitezslav Valka/SS; 211 (UP CTR), © electra/SS; 218 (LORT), © Hong Vo/SS; 222 (UPLE), © Liudmila P. Sundikova/SS; 222 (LOCTR), © Matthew Cole/SS; 223 (UPRT), © LeventeGyori/SS; 223 (UP CTR), © Ted Byrne/AL; 223 (LOCTR), Universal Stopping Point Photography/GI; 223 (UPRT), © Photomyeye/DRT; 223 (LO), © Isselee/DRT

Published by the National Geographic Society
Gary E. Knell, *President and Chief Executive Officer*
John M. Fahey, *Chairman of the Board*
Declan Moore, *Executive Vice President; President, Publishing and Travel*
Melina Gerosa Bellows, *Publisher; Chief Creative Officer, Books, Kids, and Family*

Prepared by the Book Division
Hector Sierra, *Senior Vice President and General Manager*
Nancy Laties Feresten, *Senior Vice President, Kids Publishing and Media*
Jay Sumner, *Director of Photography, Kids Publishing*
Jennifer Emmett, *Vice President, Editorial Director, Kids Books*
Eva Absher-Schantz, *Design Director, Kids Publishing and Media*
R. Gary Colbert, *Production Director*
Jennifer A. Thornton, *Director of Managing Editorial*

Staff for This Book
Kate Olesin, *Project Editor*
Jim Hiscott, Jr., *Art Director*
Jay Sumner, *Photo Editor*
Chad Tomlinson, *Designer*
Sara Zeglin, *Kids Digital Producer*
Ariane Szu-Tu, *Assistant Editor*
Paige Towler, *Editorial Assistant*
Callie Broaddus, *Associate Designer*
Carl Mehler, *Director of Maps*
Grace Hill, *Associate Managing Editor*
Joan Gossett, *Production Editor*
Lewis R. Bassford, *Production Manager*
Susan Borke, *Legal and Business Affairs*

Production Services
Phillip L. Schlosser, *Senior Vice President*
Chris Brown, *Vice President, NG Book Manufacturing*
George Bounelis, *Senior Production Manager*
Nicole Elliott, *Director of Production*
Rachel Faulise, *Manager*
Robert L. Barr, *Manager*

For Smart Bomb Interactive, Inc.
Clark Stacey, *CEO*
Jeff Amis, *VP, Product Development*
Zach Woolf, *Lead Game Designer*
Jaimee Christensen, *Art Director*
Jenna Kemker, *Lead Marketing Artist*
Scott Gwynn, *Marketing Artist*
Andrew Hernandez, *Lead Environmental Artist*
Taylor Maw, *Concept Artist*
Rose Ledezma, *Environment/Flash Artist*
Mac McCann, *Lead 3d Artist*
Laura Mercer, *3d Artist/Animator*
Tom Tolman, *Marketing Artist*
Peter Anderson, *Flash Game Artist*
Jason Keyser, *Lead EFX/Flash Artist*
Steve Fox, *Level Artist*
Lindzi Porter, *UI Artist*
Adam Hunter, *Curator/Writer*

The National Geographic Society is one of the world's largest nonprofit scientific and educational organizations. Founded in 1888 to "increase and diffuse geographic knowledge," the Society's mission is to inspire people to care about the planet. It reaches more than 400 million people worldwide each month through its official journal, *National Geographic*, and other magazines; National Geographic Channel; television documentaries; music; radio; films; books; DVDs; maps; exhibitions; live events; school publishing programs; interactive media; and merchandise. National Geographic has funded more than 10,000 scientific research, conservation, and exploration projects and supports an education program promoting geographic literacy.

For more information, please visit nationalgeographic.com, call 1-800-NGS LINE (647-5463), or write to the following address:
National Geographic Society
1145 17th Street N.W.
Washington, D.C. 20036-4688 U.S.A.

Visit us online at nationalgeographic.com/books

For librarians and teachers: ngchildrensbooks.org

More for kids from National Geographic:
kids.nationalgeographic.com

For information about special discounts for bulk purchases, please contact National Geographic Books Special Sales: ngspecsales@ngs.org

For rights or permissions inquiries, please contact National Geographic Books Subsidiary Rights: ngbookrights@ngs.org

Paperback ISBN: 978-1-4263-1778-1
Reinforced library edition ISBN: 978-1-4263-1779-8

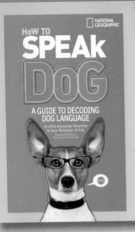

HOW TO SPEAK DOG
A GUIDE TO DECODING DOG LANGUAGE
by Aline Alexander Newman & Gary Weitzman, D.V.M.
Physician & CEO of the San Diego Humane Society

NOW THAT YOU JAM LIKE AN ANIMAL, TALK LIKE ONE!

Take your animal smarts into the real world! Learn how to communicate with your pooch in this fun guide to decoding dog language.

DOG TALK QUIZ

Test your doggie smarts! Can you match each dog's posture to the correct emotion? Fill in each box with the correct letter. (Check your answers below.)

1. **CURIOUS** "Whuzzup?"

2. **SUBMISSIVE** "Just tell me what you want. You're the boss!"

3. **LONELY** "I'm all alone. Where did everybody go?"

4. **PLAYFUL** "Throw me the ball!"

5. **AFRAID** "I'll do anything you want. Please don't hurt me."

6. **AGGRESSIVE** "Back off, now—before somebody gets hurt!"

Belgian shepherd

Border collie

German short-haired pointer

Border collie

Wire fox terrier

Dachshund

Answers: 1.C, 2.D, 3.E, 4.B, 5.B, 6.A

12

13

NO DOG? NO PROBLEM!

Discover more awesome books about all kinds of amazing creatures.

MISSION: LION RESCUE
ALL ABOUT LIONS AND HOW TO SAVE THEM

MISSION: WOLF RESCUE
ALL ABOUT WOLVES AND HOW TO SAVE THEM

125 True Stories of Amazing Animals

125 True Stories of Amazing Pets

© 2014 National Geographic Society

NATIONAL GEOGRAPHIC KIDS

AVAILABLE WHEREVER BOOKS ARE SOLD
and at nationalgeographic.com/books

f Like us on Facebook: Nat Geo Books
Follow us on Twitter: @NatGeoBooks